BORN TO WIN
FIND YOUR SUCCESS CODE

Books on Personality Development

BORN TO WIN

FIND YOUR SUCCESS CODE

ZIG ZIGLAR
&
TOM ZIGLAR

PRABHAT PAPERBACKS

Published by
PRABHAT PAPERBACKS
4/19 Asaf Ali Road,
New Delhi-110 002 (INDIA)
e-mail: prabhatbooks@gmail.com

Published in arrangement with Ziglar Inc., Texas, USA

ISBN 978-93-5186-974-0
BORN TO WIN
by Zig Ziglar & Tom Ziglar

Edition
2020

Price
₹ 200.00 (Rupees Two Hundred only)

Printed at
R-Tech Offset Printers, Delhi

PRAISE FOR BORN TO WIN

"Buy *Born to Win* before your competition does! Imagine sitting at the feet of one of the greatest teachers of all time. *Born to Win* gives you that opportunity. Success defined from A to Ziglar. *Born to Win*; read to win!"

—Michael J. Maher
Author of *(7L) The Seven Levels of Communication*
America's most referred real estate professional
LinkedIn.com's most endorsed professional

"As he has for so many thousands of other people, Zig has positively changed my life. In this book he delivers to you, in concentrated form, the best of the best 'Ziglar Gold' that his entire family and team have created over the past forty years. Read it and be encouraged by the world's greatest encourager, Zig Ziglar, to have your life transformed!"

—Rory Vaden
Co-Founder of Southwestern Consulting
and author of *Take the Stairs*

"Zig Ziglar is one of a kind. My life—and the lives of millions—is better in every way because of the influence and example of this incredible man!"

—Andy Andrews
New York Times best-selling author of *The Traveler's Gift*

"If I could recommend only two books to help you become more, do more, and have more, the first would be the Bible; the second is *Born to Win*. This masterpiece makes it clear why Zig Ziglar has been the world's great motivator for five decades."

—Dave Anderson
President of LearnToLead
Author of *How to Lead by THE BOOK*

"I have read over five hundred books on life, success, winning, sales, and personal development over the past twenty-one years, but *Born to Win* is the only book that will sit on my desk. I will read it every day, reading a few paragraphs as a daily refresher or entire chapters to enhance my skills. *Born to Win* is one of the ten books everyone should own and read. No wonder titans of world business, politics, and sports consider Zig Ziglar to be the single greatest influence in their lives—and I am no exception. Equally as important are the millions of people around the globe who have experienced the life-changing wisdom of this living legend; a living legend that guided this former British solider from failure to success, from poverty to prosperity, and from insignificance to significance. The advice, content, and material in *Born to Win* are quite literally priceless; it is the culmination of a lifetime's work. If you are ready to become the person you were born to be (a Ziglarpreneur), buy it, read it, reread it, and apply it. Do it today, as it's never the wrong time to do the right thing!"

—Andy T. Hansen, FInstSMM
UK's number-one motivational speaker
Sales trainer
Life coach

"Zig has done it again! The hope, inspiration, and proven principles we have come to expect from the world's premier motivational teacher!"

—David Horsager
Business strategist
Author of *The Trust Edge*

"Zig Ziglar is the real deal, a life changer, an authentic voice in a wilderness of hucksters. Zig is a light, a mentor, and a model for millions."

—Seth Godin
Zig's number-one fan

"*Born to Win* is a tremendous testament to the importance of balanced success—something that is so easy to miss in life. Zig Ziglar not only addresses the importance of mental preparation and the behavior commitments necessary to accomplish your goals, he inspires you to want to be better as you read this, no matter how successful you already have been. This is a fantastic book."

—Joe Takash
President of Victory Consulting

"I've been listening to Zig Ziglar's teachings and reading his books since I was twelve years old. His influence and experience have permeated every business decision I've ever made, and I'm thrilled that Zig has poured all of his best insights into one book, *Born to Win*. This is absolutely a must-read for anyone in business or anyone who just wants a better life!"

—Dave Ramsey
Host of *The Dave Ramsey Show*
Best-selling author of *The Total Money Makeover*

"Zig has saved the best for last. *Born To Win* is a must-have and a must-read for anyone who wants to win in the game of life. I highly recommend it!"

—Morris "The Miracle Man" Goodman
Author and speaker

"Zig's books and tapes have been a part of our lives as long as we can remember. At ages ten and eleven, we attended our first *Born to Win* seminar. It was then that we learned how to set goals and work toward reaching those goals on a daily basis. All three of us set the goal in junior high to attend college on academic and athletic scholarships. Working our goals program on a regular basis helped us make good decisions on how to invest our time, energy, and efforts. Adam and Alex went to Abilene Christian University on full ride ride golf/academic scholarships and Luke joined us in the fall of 2010 with his own full ride golf/academic scholarship.

Zig's motivational talks constantly helped us stay focused on our big goals. A *Born to Win* attitude and developing strong relationships have helped us accomplish so many of our goals. If you practice what Zig talks about, you too will be able to achieve more than you ever imagined. Who would have dreamed that Alex, at age twenty, would play in his first PGA tour event? Adam has experienced success on and off the golf course, with numerous state and collegiate golf victories while maintaining a 4.0 GPA. Finally, Luke, at age seventeen, won the Arkansas Overall State High School Championship and multiple other academic high school honors. Mr. Ziglar, we are proud and thankful for your input into our personal lives."

—Adam, Alex, and Luke Carpenter

FOREWORD

I met Larry Carpenter for the first time in 1981 when he attended my Born to Win seminar in Dallas, Texas. Following that seminar, Larry moved to Dallas to attend Dallas Baptist University, where I served on the Board of Directors. Every Sunday, Larry was on the front row of my Sunday school class, usually with three or four of his college buddies. Little did I realize what a fixture Larry would become and how significant my friendship with him would be through the years. From 1981 to 2007, Larry attended my Born to Win seminar at least once a year (many times with his wife, Lisa, and their three sons, plus more than one hundred of his employees and friends).

At the final Born to Win seminar, which was held in 2007, I presented Larry with my chrome-handled pump, which I had used at my live presentations for more than thirty years. The story of the pump signifies persistence and dedication to hard work and specific goals, which Larry had personified throughout our thirty-year friendship. When I considered whom to ask to write the foreword to this book, there was only one name that came to mind: my student and my friend, Larry Carpenter.

The first year I met Zig Ziglar was in 1981. I had been given a copy of his book *See You at the Top* by one of my best friends, Bobby Spain. Bobby had watched me struggle in an attempt to break away from a blue-collar work and home environment and suggested my solution would lie in the hands and philosophy of Zig's Born to Win seminar, taking place in Dallas, Texas. So, I signed up! I realized I needed help, but had no idea my entire perspective on life would change in just four days.

Zig had studied and learned from many of the great ones, like Earl Nightingale, Dale Carnegie, and many others. Zig often told me his research always included a thorough physiological, psychological, and theological review before he felt comfortable sharing his own principles of success. This statement provided me, as it should you, an additional level of comfort and trust—a trust he has never broken in our thirty-year relationship.

Zig Ziglar is the most skilled professional in communications I have ever read, heard, or met, and today he is my friend as well as my mentor. Within hours of my first encounter with Zig, he began challenging me. Zig told me I was *"designed for accomplishment, engineered for success, and endowed with the seeds of greatness."* Right from the very beginning I hit it off with him. The "one-on-one" special moments of personal attention at that first Born to Win seminar seemed to be a divine destiny, and his messages on CDs forever changed my life. It was later I learned that he'd often speak to twenty-five to thirty thousand people at huge events, but at that time the only one I was aware of... was me!

Zig told me there are three things you simply can't do: you can't push a rope, you can't put toothpaste back in a tube, and you can't saw sawdust. The first thing I had to learn was a willingness to let go of the past. Zig taught me that the key to success was centered in the pursuit of action-oriented goals, and I totally bought into Zig's goal-setting philosophy. His seven-step process is incredibly designed with pinpoint accuracy for *you*, the fortunate reader of this book. I slept with Zig's Performance Planner under my pillow for three years, accomplished more than two hundred major goals, and accumulated substantial wealth as the result of taking his advice and implementing his principles.

I can assure you that Zig's *Born to Win* philosophy really does work, and I especially appreciate the balanced approach to life that Born to Win teaches. Along with financial wealth, I enjoy good health, a terrific love of my family, and the spiritual peace of mind that only a life of no regrets can offer. I have a deep sense of joy living with Lisa, my beautiful, creative wife of twenty-five years, and my three handsome, energetic sons round out my family heritage.

I read this book as it was a work in progress, and I've lived and breathed Zig's philosophy: "*You can have everything in life you want, if you will just help enough other people get what they want.*" This process works! This philosophy is true! And the legend and legacy of Zig Ziglar continues. As you pick up this book, within the first forty pages the magic, inspiration, and dream of living a life that is simply awesome will suddenly manifest itself through your own personality. Good luck, and buckle in for a 7,500-horsepower "fast read" that is totally worth the scare of the ride.

—Larry R. Carpenter
President and CEO
Carpenter Hotel Group, LLC

This book is dedicated to all who understand
that they were made not with a spirit of timidity,
but with a spirit of power and self-discipline.
They are, in fact, Born to Win!

Contents

PART THREE: EXPECTING TO WIN

PREFACE

ZIGLAR PURE AND SIMPLE

The *Born to Win* philosophy is both "profoundly simple" and "simply profound." The concept that you have to plan to win and prepare to win before you can expect to win is simple, but simple doesn't mean it's necessarily easy, and when you dig a little deeper, you understand just how profound it really is.

In my career at Ziglar (I tell people I have been in the business for forty-six years, since I am forty-six years old), I have worked with many individuals and companies who are seeking a higher level of success. One of my previous roles in the company was to market "success" seminars. Through the years we have come up with many interesting and compelling seminar titles and marketing headlines. The idea in a headline is to make it state exactly what the prospects really want so that they take action right away. The following headline is my all-time favorite, although for obvious reasons we never used it:

"Success the Easy Way in 5 Minutes or Less—GUARANTEED! Or Double Your Money Back."

Yep, that pretty much sums up what almost every individual and company is looking for! The bad news is there are no "magic pill" solutions that allow you to achieve success "fast and easy."

However, there are several success strategies that will allow you to achieve a higher level of success faster and more easily than you thought was possible—and that is what this book is about, to give you a road map for success in pure and simple language. Don't get me wrong, winning doesn't come without work, but focusing on the proven steps and processes to winning will allow the journey to be faster and a ton more fun.

TWO WORDS AND A PHRASE

In order to keep things simple (just the way my mind likes it!), I want to share with you two words and a phrase that I use as key points when I explain to people how to achieve consistent and lasting success.

Two Words: Identity and Hope

For many years I wondered why Dad has been so successful at motivating people to change, to take action, to try something different or new. Growing up, I thought it was because he was so inspirational, funny, and smart. What Dad says makes sense, and nobody says it better than he does! Yet all of these things only explain why people like him, not why they take action. I know trust has a lot to do with it, yet many people hear him only one time and then are inspired to take action. Sure, the foundation for trust was established, but something more than trust had to move them to action.

Digging a little deeper and asking the "why" question (*Why do people take action?*), I discovered this scarlet thread. Almost every time Dad speaks, and in almost every book, tape, CD, video, or DVD he has done, he tells *his* story. In a nutshell, Dad's story goes like this: Born in the heart of the Depression, he was the tenth of twelve children. His dad died when he was five. Dad started working at age six, never did well in school, married when he was twenty. He started his sales career and failed miserably for several years. An executive at his company told him he could be a champion if only he believed in himself and went to work on a regular schedule. He had always been honest and worked hard, but with this new information he changed his attitude, and his sales career started to take off. Unfortunately, while he would achieve momentary success over the next twenty years, he was still chasing the worldly definition of success and looking for the "get rich quick" solution. Because of this, he found himself having to start over more than ten times during that twenty-year stretch. Stability was not a word to describe Dad! Then, when Dad was forty-five years old, his life totally changed as he discovered his eternal purpose with his faith in Christ. The rest is history.

Something very interesting happens when Dad tells his story. You start to see people's heads nodding. If you could read their minds, this is what you would see: "Wow! I had no idea Zig struggled so much when he was coming up. His dad died when he was five. His mom had a fifth-grade education. He didn't do well in school. When he started in sales, he was horrible.

"He made and lost money numerous times because of really bad decisions. *Wow, if Zig did it, so can I.*" Suddenly they identify with Dad, and hope is born.

Inspiration is powerful, and Dad may be the most inspirational person on the planet, but inspiration only lasts so long. Hope is much different. When you have the hope that things can change and a plan to make that change possible, then you can take action. When Dad tells his story, it literally flips the hope switch in people because they identify with him—"If he can, I can."

Now, all of a sudden when Dad suggests that people try something, they do it—not because they like Dad, or because he inspired them or made them laugh, but because "if he can, I can."

Next time you get discouraged and caught up in your circumstances, just remember what Dad says: "You cannot control what happens to you, but you can control how you respond to what happens to you." If he can, YOU can.

A PHRASE: WILL, SKILL, AND REFILL

My simple mind really loves this phrase: Will, Skill, and Refill. Almost every day I get asked the question, "What are the keys to constantly improving my personal or my company's level of success?" As Dad says, "You build a better company by building better people," so the Will, Skill, and Refill philosophy is a foundation of all of our personal and corporate training. This is how it works:

Will—this is the "want to." This is the heart, the desire, the attitude, the passion that people have.

Skill—this is the "how to." This is the skill, the process, the technical expertise that people have.

Refill—this is reinforcing the Will and Skill. There is no such thing as "one and done" training and development. Will and Skill must be developed and reinforced daily. Take the Will away from any person and you will have at best someone who is just taking up space, and at worst someone who is a real drain on their company and their family. Without Skill, no matter what you do, you will create an endless cycle of frustration. Without Refill it is impossible to maintain the difference-making levels of Will and Skill you need to achieve the level of success you desire.

BE WEIRD!

I love what Dave Ramsey says about being in debt. He says that "normal" people are broke, so be weird. I agree 100 percent! As Dad says, "I have had problems when I have had money, and I have had problems when I haven't had money, and I have discovered that if you are going to have problems, it's better if you have money!"

Here is the reality: "normal" people are not successful in the truest sense of the word. "Normal" people do not practice Will, Skill, and Refill. I am encouraging you to BE WEIRD. Choosing to be successful starts with choosing to do what successful people do. Successful people practice Will, Skill, and Refill on a daily basis.

Will, Skill, and Refill is simple—remember, I am a simple person, so it has to be! This concept is based on my favorite of all of Dad's quotes: *"You are who you are and what you are because of what has gone into your mind. You can change who you are and what you are by changing what goes into your mind."*

> "YOU ARE WHO YOU ARE AND WHAT YOU ARE BECAUSE OF WHAT HAS GONE INTO YOUR MIND. YOU CAN CHANGE WHO YOU ARE AND WHAT YOU ARE BY CHANGING WHAT GOES INTO YOUR MIND."

Here is how you do it. On a daily basis, even if it is only for five or ten minutes a day, Refill your mind with material that helps you build your Will, or your Skill, or both. You can read or listen to great material. This book is a great place to start, and as you are reading this very sentence you are practicing Will, Skill, and Refill. Dad's favorite example of Will, Skill, and Refill is Automobile University. When you are driving, pop in a powerful CD that builds you up.

Personally, I have loaded my iPod with hundreds of hours of life-building material (of course my favorite is Dad) and I listen almost every time I work out.

There is no such thing as the "status quo." Coasting in life, in business, or in your family relationships is not an option. All are either improving or getting worse. The same is true for success. You are either moving closer to success, or further from it. This is why Will, Skill, and Refill are so critical on a daily basis.

"Encouragement is the fuel on which hope runs."

—Zig Ziglar

As you plan, prepare, and expect to win in life because you are *born to win*, never forget that hope is the catalyst that will get you started, and that encouragement keeps hope alive. The daily dose of Will, Skill, and Refill is where you will find encouragement. Remember, you were Born to Win! Prepare Yourself! Expect Success! Change the World!

—Tom Ziglar

ACKNOWLEDGMENTS

Thank you, Jean Abernathy Ziglar (Sugar Baby), for being the only girl I've ever loved and for believing I was born to win even when I hadn't yet realized it for myself.

Thank you to my children, Tom Ziglar, Cindy Ziglar, and Julie Ziglar Norman, my granddaughter Katherine Lemons, and my son-in-law Jim Norman for helping me bring this book to press. It is my joy to work with my family.

Thank you, Laurie Magers, my executive assistant for over thirty-four years, for being dedicated to making this book the best it can be and for always doing everything with great care and professionalism.

Thank you, Billy Cox, my longtime friend, Ziglar, Inc., board member, and exceptional business entrepreneur, for the incredible amount of time and effort you put into helping me make the content of this book all that it needed to be.

Thank you, my friend Larry Carpenter, for writing the foreword of this book, for serving on the Ziglar, Inc., Advisory Board, and for being the person who attended my Born to Win course more often than any other! You have always championed the Born to Win philosophy, and you live the philosophy more completely than anyone I have ever met. Your success in life and in business are proof that you were born to win!

Thank you, Michael Levin, my new friend, for editing my book with a heart of true understanding about my goals for my reader. Your insight was spot-on and your input added untold value to the content.

Thank you to my Ziglar, Inc., team! You make my work sustainable and I am happily indebted to you!

Many thanks to all of you who have read one of my books or heard me speak, applied what you learned, and discovered that you, too, were born to win! This book is a result of your success in applying these principles.

My deepest gratitude is for the One who has directed my life since July 4, 1972: my Lord and Savior, Jesus Christ. Because of my relationship with Him, my mind and heart are free of fear and worry, and I can look forward in excited anticipation for what is yet to come.

INTRODUCTION

In November of 2011, I celebrated the sixty-fourth anniversary of my twenty-first birthday, and I'm still busier than a one-armed man calling on twin sisters! I'm still working on new books and encouraging people everywhere I go. I love every minute of it. Lots of people say they heard I have retired! I always exclaim, "You heard wrong! You should have heard I was 're-fired.' I'm not going to ease up, let up, shut up, or give up until I'm taken up. As a matter of fact, I'm just getting warmed up."

However, when you get to be my age, you think back over your life and consider how effective you may have been and what you did that made the biggest difference in people's lives. For me that is an easy answer. In my own life, my conversion to Christ and my marriage made the biggest difference for me. As for the things I did that had the greatest impact on the lives of others, the first is providing audio products for people to listen to in their cars. I've always been an advocate of "Automobile University," and through the years I've received hundreds of pounds of mail from people telling me how they take me with them every day in their daily commute and on business trips. I'm always tickled that I can go just about anywhere and very few people recognize my face, but when I open my mouth and start talking, heads turn, and often I'm asked if I am Zig Ziglar. My voice is distinctive, and when you combine it with my Yazoo City, Mississippi, accent, well, it's not really stepping out on a limb when folks guess that it's me.

The second effective thing I've done is a three-day seminar I offered several times a year for more than thirty years. Originally, the seminar was called "The Richer Life Course," but eventually it became known as simply "Born to Win." Through the years I've come to know thousands of people whose lives were transformed materially and spiritually as a result of participating in the Born to Win experience.

> YOU WERE BORN TO WIN, BUT TO BE THE WINNER YOU WERE BORN TO BE, YOU HAVE TO PLAN TO WIN AND PREPARE TO WIN. THEN AND ONLY THEN CAN YOU EXPECT TO WIN.

Possibly you, my friend, have contributed to the stack of mail I've gotten these past forty-plus years. I am so grateful for folks like you who have shared what has been most important and significant to them. As I previously mentioned, the Born to Win seminar and my audio products head the lists, but why have they been so effective? What was being taught in those activities that has had such a powerful impact on people's lives? The answer to that question is in the words I've used to describe the Born to Win experience: *"You were born to win, but to be the winner you were born to be, you have to plan to win and prepare to win. Then and only then can you expect to win."* The "Ziglar Gold" is found in principles and techniques I have taught people that show them how to plan, prepare, and expect to win. This may not sound earth-shaking, but you must understand that these skills and attitudes have the power to transform your life.

My own life was transformed by these principles more than fifty years ago by some tough comments made by one of my mentors, my area sales supervisor, Mr. P. C. Merrell. I will share more of my experience with Mr. Merrell later in the book. However, through his instruction and lots of mentoring from others, I learned the power of planning, preparing, and expecting to win. When I learned how to plan each day and set specific goals, I became more focused on the things that really make a difference. When I learned how to prepare myself and equip myself with the tools and skills I needed to be successful, I was able to execute my plans and turn them into winning results. Finally, when I learned how to expect success, it all came together and transformed my life and the life of my family. All this to say that Ziglar Gold is captured when you acquire the skill set needed to plan, prepare, and expect to win.

I've always considered myself to be a professional "encourager," and my mission was to help people find hope when there didn't seem to be any. To fulfill that role, I've always tried to give people lots of simple ideas that will help them change the way they think about themselves. As I look back over my career I see that just about everything I taught really can be categorized as planning, preparing, or expecting to win. Because of that, I have organized this book into three sections that track the best stories, ideas, and principles that relate to those skills. When you finish reading *Born to Win*, you will have the absolutely very best of the core principles and skills I have shared with people for the past forty-plus years. Let me give you a quick preview of what you will learn in *Born to Win*.

PART I: PLANNING TO WIN

There are lots of parts and sub-parts you have to put together when you begin to plan your success, but a few things are foundational. Planning has to be based on getting a clear **vision** of what you want, because without a vision you don't know which **goals** to set. Without goals you have no targets, and without targets you have nothing to **measure** how you're doing. So you can see how important a vision is. Getting a clear vision for your future is also important because it plays a huge role in the creation of *desire*! Did you know that desire is the mother of motivation? **Desire** is the "want to" and the motor that fuels and powers sustained success.

Desire is important and vision is critical, but there are some personal qualities you must have or acquire to get the best possible results. As a matter of fact, there are six qualities: *honesty, character, faith, integrity, love,* and loyalty. I have called these qualities the foundation stones in the stairway to the top. You are going to learn how these qualities are critical and how to implement them as you plan to win.

PART II: PREPARING TO WIN

At first glance, you might think planning and preparing mean the same thing. I admit they might look like they are first cousins, but I see preparation as much different from planning. Preparation is a matter of equipping yourself to win with the right tools, knowledge, and support it will take to turn your dreams into plans that will make your vision into reality. So, this section of *Born to Win* will be about how to equip yourself in the best possible way to ensure your planning efforts will be successful.

- You need the right knowledge to win.
- You must continually raise your personal performance bar.
- You must acquire tools that help you work better and faster.

- You have to practice your skills.
- You have to surround yourself with positive influences and people.

In summary, you have to train yourself to become a twenty-four-hour champion. Winning involves planning and preparing. Both are a constant-improvement, never-ending process. When you stop planning and preparing... you stop winning. Twenty-four-hour champions continually equip themselves to win!

PART III: EXPECTING TO WIN

I've always said that when you have planned and prepared to win, you then have the *right* to expect to win. This section of *Born to Win* is going to show you the power of expectation and what drives it! The ultimate fruit of positive expectation is hope, and it is hope that pulls you forward in all you attempt to do. I'm always hopeful and I never worry. I can say that because I expect the best possible result in all that I do. I expect the best because I planned my success, prepared myself to execute my plans, and earned the right to expect the best.

Desire is the mother of motivation because that is where your motivation is born. Properly planning and preparing heightens your expectations, which fuels your desire and drives you to become even more motivated. Through the years I've continually heard from individuals from all walks of life whose lives were in a downward spiral—until they heard something in my audio products or read something in my books that gave them the will and the skills they needed to change their

> DESIRE IS THE MOTHER OF MOTIVATION BECAUSE THAT IS WHERE YOUR MOTIVATION IS BORN.

circumstances and transform their lives. They testify that by putting my simple suggestions into practice their lives were transformed. Sometimes the transformation was mental, sometimes it was spiritual, and other times it was material. Whatever the transformation, there was a commonality to the core changes they made. These people changed the way they viewed themselves. They became willing to make significant changes, and they came to believe they were *born to win*! What they really did is develop the skills and take the necessary actions they needed to plan, prepare, and expect to win!

My son Tom and I are co-authors of this book. Together we chose the most effective information I have taught in twenty-nine books over the past forty years. After you've read this book and Tom's contributions, I believe you will see why I have faith that the Ziglar legacy, along with our pure and simple philosophy, is in good hands for the generations to come. I'm not the kind of guy who says anything is over until it's over, but because of my age, it's possible that this book may be my last. This is why I have dotted every "i" and crossed every "t" in this book to make sure it contains the very best of the best of all I've learned and taught in my career. I do believe you were born to win. But I also know that to be the winner you were born to be, you have to plan to win and prepare to win before you can expect to win. There are a lot of things that have to happen before you can change the world!

—Zig Ziglar

Part One

Planning to Win

CHAPTER ONE

WANTING TO WIN

I've always said that man was *designed for accomplishment, engineered for success, and endowed with the seeds of greatness.* I believe that almost as much as I believe in God. What I mean when I make that statement is that man has the opportunity to achieve greatness and is hard-wired to make it happen. Every person has unique gifts, and those gifts give him or her the power and the opportunity to accomplish great things, if he or she learns how to use those gifts and channel them in the right direction. Now you might say, "Zig, if that's true, why doesn't everyone achieve greatness?" Actually, that answer is easy. Everybody doesn't want to be great, and many people who want to be great aren't willing to do the work to make it possible!

The great coach of the Green Bay Packers, Vince Lombardi, wisely stated, "Winning isn't everything but wanting to win is." The simple truth is that you have to want to do something badly enough before you have the slightest chance of doing it! If you don't want it badly enough, I absolutely guarantee that you will not be willing to do the planning and preparing it takes to get it.

Psychologists will tell you in a New York minute (which, for your information, is thirty-two seconds) that you invariably and inevitably move toward the strongest impression in your mind. The impressions that are most vivid in your mind are the things you want to do. That's why desire is so powerful and plays a big role in planning. If you really want to do something, it means that it's something you are going to think about most of the time. When you constantly think about something, you talk about it all the time and you get lots of new ideas about how to make it happen. When you have lots of ideas about something, it makes planning easier and more enjoyable. Desire also makes you willing to become accountable for your plan, and that makes you more willing to create the plan you need to win.

DESIRE IS THE MOTHER OF MOTIVATION

In my first book, *See You at the Top*, I said, "Desire is the ingredient that changes the hot water of mediocrity to the steam of outstanding success." What this means is that desire is the catalyst that enables a person with average ability to compete and win against others with more natural talent. You see, my friend, being a winner is much different from having the potential to win. Everyone has the potential; it's what you do with that potential that really matters. Nothing is more inspiring than a person with seemingly mediocre talent rising against the odds to become a champion by way of hard work, effort, and perseverance toward their goals. Obviously, raw talent is important, but the difference-maker between first and the rest of the pack is usually desire.

> DESIRE IS THE INGREDIENT THAT CHANGES THE HOT WATER OF MEDIOCRITY TO THE STEAM OF OUTSTANDING SUCCESS.

I've spent my life studying, thinking, teaching, living, and sharing motivation. I've learned why some people do better than others. As a matter of fact, I've now written thirty books on the subject that have been translated into forty different languages and dialects, and I've spoken to thousands of audiences in front of millions of people. The Ziglar team has created more than fifty audio programs and hundreds of customized audio presentations through the years. I'm grateful that I have been able to see so many lives transformed through these various methods of communication. My core philosophy on winning and motivation is summed up by saying that you were *born to win*, but in order to be the winner you were born to be, you have to plan to win and prepare to win before you can expect to win. The playing field of life is not level, and for you to compete in the game of life, you need an equalizer of some kind. In the old West, the equalizer was the six-shooter. It enabled a little guy to chop a bigger man down to size.

Desire is also an equalizer—and nowadays is highly encouraged over a six-shooter! Desire creates an edge. Desire produces the energy to get out of bed when you don't feel like it. Desire gives you the power to run the last one hundred yards of a marathon when you think even one more step is impossible! Desire gives you the will to do the tough things your competition may not be willing to do. Desire is the mother of motivation, because it is where motivation is born. Desire will pull you across the finish line and give you victory!

There are two questions you might ask at this point: how is desire created, and what does it have to do with planning to win? Since I'm here to help you with the hard ones, I'm going to answer both of those questions in this chapter.

DESIRE IS BORN WITH VISION

To understand how desire connects with planning, you have to understand how desire is created. Desire is created when something happens in your life that suddenly

> DESIRE IS CREATED WHEN SOMETHING HAPPENS IN YOUR LIFE THAT SUDDENLY CHANGES THE WAY YOU SEE YOURSELF IN RELATIONSHIP TO YOUR FUTURE.

changes the way you see yourself in relationship to your future. We all have moments in our lives that are turning points—crossroads where something happens that can shape the direction of our future. Some of these turning points can be dramatic, and others may be subtle. I want to encourage you to be looking for these turning points and seeking out your purpose and passion as you engage in the planning, preparing, and expecting to win process.

I vividly remember the exact day one of these turning points happened in my professional life. I was one of twelve children raised by a single, widowed mother in Yazoo City, Mississippi, during the Great Depression. We struggled and worked hard to make ends meet, and although we never had a lot of 'extra' things, we always had what we needed. When I was a young boy I worked around our little home doing chores, and when I was nine I got a job at a grocery store in town. At that point in my life I saw myself as a little guy from a little town who would always live in Yazoo City. That type of thinking was the result of my experience growing up. I had no idea that other possibilities might exist for me. I entertained the idea of owning my own store, or meat market to be exact, but I never really felt over-the-top excited about it. I wasn't excited about it because it was not my vision—it was just an idea that was presented to me by my boss as a possibility. You might say I was a wandering generality instead of a meaningful specific. I was wandering around with no direction and no plan to win.

After I grew up and married my beautiful Redhead, Jean Abernathy (whom I call "Sugar Baby"), I got a job as a door-to-door salesman in the cookware industry. The first two-and-a-half years I sold a lot—I sold our furniture, our china and silver, the dog... just kidding. But it was no joking matter that we struggled financially and were in hot water all the time. One cold, snowy morning I went to a meeting where Mr. P.C. Merrell, the divisional supervisor from Tennessee, took an interest in me. Mr. Merrell said, "Zig, you have the ability to be a great one." Frankly, I'd never heard words like that. As a child raised during the Depression, the emphasis was on survival—not being "great." Now here was a man for whom I had the utmost respect, a man who was my hero, a man of integrity, and he was emphatic that he really believed I could be the best cookware salesman in the country. But he also had some constructive criticism. He said, "You know, Zig, I've been watching you for two-and-a-half years and I have never seen such a waste." (Now, friends, that will get your attention!) Somewhat startled, I asked what he meant. He explained, "You have a lot of ability. You could be a great one and maybe even become a national champion." Naturally, I was flattered, but a little skeptical, so I asked if he really meant it. He assured me, "Zig, there is no doubt in my mind if you really went to work on an organized schedule and started believing in yourself, you could go all the way to the top."

Mr. Merrell's words gave me hope that I could change and caused me to believe for the first time in my life that maybe I did have more to offer than I'd ever realized. Looking back, Mr. Merrell's words helped me make the decisions that changed my life. I turned his words over and over in my mind and got more excited by the minute. On that day, for the first time in my life, I suddenly had a clear vision of a future I really wanted, and I also noticed that something else was building inside of me. It was desire... the desire to make it happen started to build! Mr. Merrell planted a seed when he told me I could be great at something, and I believed him. My vision of my future started to change immediately, and I wanted that new future. As my desire grew I became sick and tired of being sick and tired. I wanted to change, and more important, I felt empowered to turn that new vision into reality. I took immediate action.

You may be reading this book and thinking, "Zig, I don't have a Mr. Merrell in my life." Yes, you do. I am your Mr. Merrell. I honestly believe I have felt your feelings, I've walked in your shoes. You have made some mistakes, and you may not be where you want to be, but that has nothing to do with your future. I'll say it again and again: you can start from where you are with what you've got and go to where it is you want to go. Yes, you were literally *born to win*. My goal is to give you new hope in this game of life and turn that new hope into a brilliant new picture for your future. I want you to know that when you prepare yourself, you can expect success.

> YOU CAN START FROM WHERE YOU ARE WITH WHAT YOU'VE GOT AND GO TO WHERE IT IS YOU WANT TO GO.

Many decades have passed since Mr. Merrell's empowering words gave me a new vision for my life and the powerful desire to become what he said I could be. I see looking back that even though we may have a vision and a strong desire to attain it, seeing the end of it is not always possible. We can only see so far, because our experience limits us. But I also learned that we should embrace the vision and fuel our desire. As we work with purpose and pursue our passion we will be able to see farther, and when we get there we'll be able to see farther again!

In my case, I first had a vision of becoming a national sales champion, and I accomplished that in a few short years. In the process of accomplishing that goal, I developed another vision that was even more powerful. I wanted to become a public speaker. That turned out pretty well, too.

COMMITMENT AND PERSEVERANCE ARE POWERED BY DESIRE

If you could somehow count all the books that have been written on what it takes to be successful, the number would be astronomical. A significant number of those books (including several I have written) emphasize the importance of taking action on the ideas and opportunities that present themselves in life. The fact is that you can have lots of good ideas and you can be exposed to many great opportunities, but if you don't do something about them, they might as well be non-existent. It's pretty amazing how most people put off taking the necessary actions to acquire the things they want and then complain about how they never get a break! There are many reasons people find to justify not taking action, but the absence of desire is one of the root causes. They just really don't *want* it badly enough. This is a fatal condition when you are trying to be successful.

We all know that life is tough. Many times our best plans turn sour as we pursue our goals and dreams. For that reason, there are two qualities every person must have to fuel their desire and sustain their pursuit of success. Those two qualities are commitment and perseverance. You need commitment to produce the focus and consistency you need to keep your eye on the target. Then you need perseverance to make it over the rough spots and setbacks you will most certainly experience along your journey to success.

Commitment is the solution to help you overcome the distractions you will face in life and help you stay focused on what really matters. Today, most of our society is up to their necks in the Internet and all that comes with it. Don't get me wrong. I think the information we now have at our fingertips is astounding, and information is a key ingredient in being informed and equipped with the knowledge we need for success. But the level of information in this day and time is far more than any one person can possibly handle and process. You might say we live in a time of "information overload." The result of information overload is usually distraction, and it dilutes your focus and takes you off your game.

In golf, if you take your eye off the ball, you will flub it, top it, slice it, hook it, or maybe miss it entirely. Information overload has the same effect. It can cause us to take our eye off the small things we need to consistently do in order to get the results we need. Commitment is about binding ourselves to a specific course of action. People who are committed realize that they have to do specific things to get specific results and they know the results they want. Simply stated, commitment—which is fueled by desire—helps us stay on track to achieve our goals and ultimately win.

SIMPLY STATED, COMMITMENT—WHICH IS FUELED BY DESIRE—HELPS US STAY ON TRACK TO ACHIEVE OUR GOALS AND ULTIMATELY WIN.

Many of you may have heard me tell the story of how I was a boxer earlier in life, but I had to quit because of my hands. The referee kept stepping on them. When Muhammad Ali fought George Foreman in 1974 for the heavyweight championship of the world, he used a strategy he called "Rope a Dope." Ali leaned on the ropes, covered his head, and let Foreman pound on him for seven rounds in hopes that Foreman's superior strength and punching power would be exhausted and make him vulnerable to Ali's speed and quickness. I don't know about you, but the idea of letting someone like George Foreman hit me repeatedly is pretty frightening—and I'd feel that way before he threw his first punch at me. After he actually started pounding on me, I might have second thoughts about maintaining the strategy! But Ali did maintain the strategy, and it paid off for him in round eight when Foreman was so worn out from pounding on Ali he could hardly hold his arms up. Ali suddenly came off the ropes and landed two rights and a massive left hook that sent Foreman to the canvas. Perseverance on the part of Ali had carried him through to victory in one of the greatest fights in history.

Many times as we go through life, we get pounded on just like Ali did in the ring that night with big George Foreman. When tough times happen, we have to persevere through those difficulties and keep pressing on to our ultimate goal and vision. When we get knocked down, we have to get back up and keep on fighting... we must stay focused and remember our greatest victories are still ahead.

More often than not, too many people give up when they get more resistance than they bargained for. Things just seem to get a lot tougher and more difficult than they are willing to deal with. If they fail to persevere through those times, they will fail permanently! If you don't finish something, it won't be complete, and until something is completed, it isn't finished. Much about success is just the result of simply the ability to follow up, follow through, and finish what we started. You're not beaten by being knocked down. You're only beaten if you stay down.

Personally, I believe I quit my sales career (in my own mind) more times than anybody who will ever read this book has thought about quitting. It was discouraging to be broke, in debt, uncertain of what I was doing, and not really knowing from one day to the next whether I would sink or swim. It's times like that when faith, hope, courage, dedication, and persistence are of the utmost importance.

I'll have to admit it was tough, and discouragement was a frequent companion of mine. I often had to buy fifty cents' worth of gasoline at a time, and if I made a mistake in addition, I would have to place one or two items at the grocery store back on the shelf. I've had my lights and telephone temporarily disconnected when I couldn't pay the bill, and I've even had to return a car when I could not make the payment. When our first daughter was born, the hospital bill was only sixty-four dollars. The problem was, we didn't have the sixty-four dollars. I had to make two sales in order to get the money together to pay the bill. These were all embarrassing and humiliating circumstances but, fortunately, they were not the end of the world. I had a couple of things going for me that made the difference. I was committed to what I was doing, and the desire I had to win gave me the ability to persevere through the tough times. My dream to be a professional speaker was born in 1952, and though it was not until 1970 that I could pursue my dream on a full-time basis, planning for that career began immediately.

It was 1972 before my speaking career really exploded. I was forty-five years old. However, during the course of the preparation for what was to be, I always stayed grounded in my philosophy and the principles I adhered to. I altered ways in which I delivered my message in those early years, but I was fixated on the principles because I had a powerful vision of how I could help others, and I had a powerful desire for it to become a reality. The combination of vision and desire gave me the commitment to stay the course and the perseverance to keep pursuing my dream.

DESIRE ENHANCES YOUR ABILITY TO PLAN

When you spend the time necessary to plan your future, you are actually engaged in a process that is outlining the things you need to do to fulfill your vision in life. Is there a possibility that you're not as far along in life as you would like to be? If so, do you feel it is because you're not made of the right materials and do not have the natural ability to be successful? Or is there more than just a chance that you were *born to win* but you've simply been following the wrong "blueprint" (plan of action or no plan) for your life? Obviously, I have no doubt you were *born to win*, but remember that before you can win you must plan to win and prepare to win. Then—and only then—can you expect to win. Planning to win is the first step in the winning process and, unfortunately, people resist making a plan. After all, nothing is more embarrassing than creating a plan and then failing to successfully execute the plan. You have to come up with a lot of excuses about why the plan didn't work!

Fear is the fatal killer of desire. Fear of failure is a big part of the reason why people procrastinate and avoid putting their plans in writing. Plus, planning is hard work! Desire is the difference between you being an enthusiastic planner, passionately working through all the things you need to do to be successful, or just going through the motions of planning like an item on a checklist. I hope you see that planning can either be embraced as an exciting opportunity to win, or avoided as an obligatory exercise or task. When you really want something, when you desire it and you are excited about it, you look forward to planning and preparing because you *get to do it*. The key words here are "get to do"! If you have the kind of desire I've shared with you in this chapter, planning becomes something you *get to do*, rather than something

> FEAR IS THE FATAL KILLER OF DESIRE.

you *have to do*. And we all know that we do a much better job with a "get to" attitude.

WHAT DO YOU *REALLY* WANT?

Before you go any further in the planning to win process, it's a good idea to do a desire inspection on yourself. Why? Because if you don't have a real desire to do something, your heart won't be in it. The question we need to ask ourselves is, "Why do I want to do or accomplish this?" If you are unable to answer the "why you want something" question in one simple sentence, it probably isn't a true desire of yours, so you can let go of that idea.

> IF YOU ARE UNABLE TO ANSWER THE "WHY YOU WANT SOMETHING" QUESTION IN ONE SIMPLE SENTENCE, IT PROBABLY ISN'T A TRUE DESIRE OF YOURS, SO YOU CAN LET GO OF THAT IDEA.

Weight loss is the simplest example that I can give you of how this process works. For instance, if you want to lose weight, your reasons why might be that weight loss will make you healthier, and you'll feel and look better, too. If you are clear about your vision and you really want to achieve it, you will know what you want and why you want it. When you know what you desire, you can enthusiastically create an action plan to achieve it, and you will be genuinely motivated to follow through. My friend, you already have that desire, and in the next chapter I'll show you how to take that desire and begin to win!

CHAPTER TWO
BEGIN TO WIN

If you really want to win, you have to begin. I've always agreed with what I heard my friend and fellow speaker Joe Sabah say: "You don't have to be great to get started, but you do have to start to be great." This means you have to *be* before you can *do*, and *do* before you can *have*. That probably sounds simple enough, but there is a lot more involved in that statement than you might think. That statement really captures the core issues that are connected to being successful. When you understand what these three little words (*be, do, have*) mean, you will view success in an entirely new way—and ultimately change the world!

As we look at the game of life I want to emphasize a couple of things. I believe personally that most of us have certain drives, hopes, and ambitions in life. I believe that each of us, whether we are female or male, young or old, black or white, short or tall, big or slim, have the desire to make a difference. I also believe you will agree that most people are interested in health, prosperity, happiness, friends, peace, and security.

Let me ask you a question. What is your definition of success? And do you know what success is and what it isn't? Most people think of success in terms of power or recognition or the accumulation of money and material things. They also try to define it with one sentence or capture it with one central idea. True success has more components than one sentence or idea can contain.

For years I have been using a graphic to help people "see" where they are already successful and where they need help. I call it "The Wheel of Life." I could not write this book without sharing this graph that has made such a difference in so many lives. This graph will help you "see" where you really are in the game of life. It gives you a starting point as you move forward. In other words, you have to know where you are in order to know where you're going.

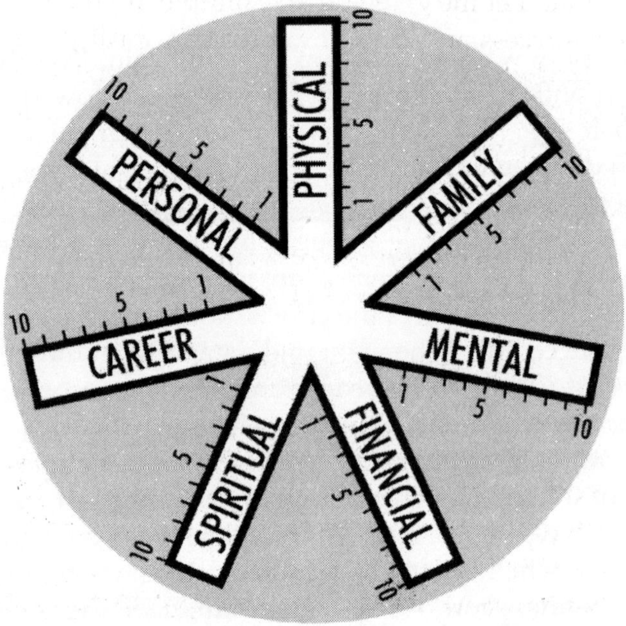

Each of the seven spokes in the wheel represents a specific area of life. The seven spokes of that wheel are:

- Physical
- Family
- Mental
- Financial
- Personal

- Spiritual
- Career

You must master some degree of success in each area of life before you can experience the true satisfaction of total success. Every spoke in your Wheel of Life is connected to the other spokes in the wheel. If one or more of the spokes is neglected, the others are also weakened. On the other hand, as you strengthen these weak areas, the other areas become stronger as well. Think of it like each area working together as a team, and the team is only as strong as its weakest link. Let me give you an example. If you just focus on career success and neglect family and spiritual growth, you will not be as successful in your professional life as you hope to be. If you make a lot of money and don't take care of your health, you might become a chronically ill wealthy person! You will clearly understand what I'm saying by understanding what success is and what it isn't. Here's a short list of the characteristics of what I believe success isn't and what I believe success is. Let's start with what success is.

WHAT SUCCESS IS:

1. Success is knowing that you did a great job when you close the door to your office at the end of each workday and head for home.
2. Success is having a home and people to love who love you in return.
3. Success is having the financial security to meet your obligations each month and the knowledge that you have provided that security for your family in the event of your demise.
4. Success is having the kind of faith that lets you know where to turn when there seems to be no place to turn.
5. Success is having an interest or hobby that gives you joy and peace.

6. Success is knowing who you are, and Whose you are.
7. Success is taking good care of you and waking up healthy each day.
8. Success is slipping under the covers at the end of the day and realizing with gratitude that, "It just doesn't get much better than this!"

You see from this list that success is more than a one-sentence definition. Success involves the whole person, and if you skimp on one area, you will limit your success in others. Now, let's take a look at what success isn't.

WHAT SUCCESS ISN'T:

1. Success isn't missing dinner with the family several times a week because of working excessively.
2. Success isn't rushing home from work and hiding out with the TV thinking, "After the day I've had, I need my space!"
3. Success isn't about how to make more money when you already have more money than you can spend.
4. Success isn't about going to church and ignoring everything you hear.
5. Success isn't all work and no play.
6. Success isn't about being so busy that you live on unhealthy fast food, served to you through little windows.
7. Success isn't spending mental energy worrying about late projects, being home on time, your health, missing your child's school play, being able to pay your bills, or finding joy in your life.
8. Success isn't texting while you drive to catch up on your overloaded schedule.

Do any of the symptoms on this list sound familiar to you? Have you noticed one or more of them in your own life? If you answered yes to any of these questions, I can tell you that your Wheel of Life needs close attention and some extra work in those areas!

YOUR RELATIONSHIP WITH YOU

As you look at the part that relationships play in your life, think about yourself. What is your relationship with yourself? Do you like who you are? If not, what are you doing about it? When I say that you have to *be* before you can *do*, and *do* before you can *have*, notice that I said *you* in front of *be, do,* and *have*. This is because I'm talking about the relationship you have with yourself and how it translates into you having the things in life that constitute success. I want to help you get acquainted with who you really are and share some things with you that will help you grow to like yourself better. It's important that you like yourself, because if you don't, who will?

Your ability to get along with other people is an indication of who you are and how you feel about yourself. You have to *be* the kind of person with whom you and others are comfortable. The more you respect yourself, the higher the standards you set and the greater your integrity, which enables you to *do* the right things. When you do the right things, you are more likely to *have* good relationships with others, and more success in general.

LAYING THE FOUNDATION

There are six characteristics that comprise the foundation stones of your life and your success. The six characteristics are honesty, character, faith, integrity, love, and loyalty. All of these foundation stones are necessary to create a Wheel of Life that is balanced and will produce the kind of success I've described. In my eighty-five years of living I have learned that people who compromise *any* of these principles usually end up with only a beggar's portion of what life offers them. I've seen people acquire money through dishonesty and deceit, but their friends are few and they lack true peace of mind. The business professional who alienates his family in his climb to the top is not a success. People who have no faith in something greater than themselves can only rely on themselves in times of great difficulty. The longer I live and the more successful people I meet, the more convinced I become that these foundation stones are the most critical success weapons you have in your arsenal.

> I ALSO WANT TO REMIND YOU THAT YOU ARE WHAT YOU ARE AND WHERE YOU ARE BECAUSE OF WHAT'S GONE INTO YOUR MIND, BUT YOU CAN CHANGE WHAT YOU ARE AND WHERE YOU ARE BY CHANGING WHAT GOES INTO YOUR MIND.

Why are these foundation stones so important to your success? Well, I'm glad you asked, because I'm going to tell you! A human being goes through life thinking and doing. Then they usually do what they think about most of the time. I want to remind you that you were *born to win*. I also want to remind you that you are *what you are and where you are because of what's gone into your mind, but you can change what you are and where you are by changing what goes into your mind*. The reason this is so is because you generally do what you think. Your thinking drives your choices. Choices determine the action you take, and action produces the results of your life. You can only think in ways consistent with the information you have in your mind. So to change what you do, you have to change the way you think, and to think differently, you need to change what goes into your mind.

Who we are is determined by the foundation stones of honesty, character, faith, integrity, love, and loyalty. The six foundational stones essentially provide the raw material for all your thinking. As such, they become the core characteristics of what you *be, do,* and *have,* which ultimately determines the results you get in life. These stones form your *code for success or failure because your thinking and your actions must be consistent with the characteristics of the foundation you build.

I wish it were possible for me to introduce you to the many personable, persuasive, talented—even brilliant—people I have met in my travels who are generally just one step in front of the bill collector and sometimes just two steps ahead of the law. They are always looking for a "deal" and the "fast buck." They *never* build very much or very high, because they have no foundation to build on. Others don't realize that *the real opportunity for success lies within the person and not in the job; that you can best get to the top by getting to the bottom of things*—and then climbing the stairs of success, one at a time. Success and happiness are not matters of chance but choice. The foundation stones provide the basis for making the right choices.

THE FOUNDATION STONES

Honesty

Many years ago, the Redhead and I went shopping for a leather sofa at a major store in town that had an enormous inventory. The salesman pleasantly approached us, we conveyed our wishes, and he led us to the sofa department. When I saw the first leather sofa that appealed to me,

---

*To find YOUR Success Code visit www.ziglar.com/borntowin.

I asked the price. He told me, and I was pleasantly shocked, because it was only about half as much as I had anticipated. When I expressed my delight that a genuine leather sofa could be bought at that price, the salesman assured me that it was indeed a remarkable buy and that was one of the reasons they sold so many of them. I told the salesman I would take it.

Next I told the salesman we needed a nice coffee table to put in front of the sofa, so we headed for the coffee table department. On the way we passed another leather sofa, very similar to the one I had just agreed to buy. If anything, I liked this one slightly better, so I walked over, looked it over carefully, sat down, leaned back, and was a little undecided as to which one I truly liked the best. So I asked the price. The salesman told me and again I was shocked, because this one was nearly twice the price of the one I had just ordered. I asked the obvious question: "Why does this one cost almost twice as much?" He explained it in one simple sentence: "This one is all leather." At that point the salesperson explained that the other sofa was mostly made of imitation leather, but nobody would ever notice it.

Which one of the sofas do you think I bought, or do you figure I walked out without buying anything? If you figured I walked out without buying anything, you hit the nail on the head. Not only did I not buy anything that day, but I have never been back in the store. The salesperson had been dishonest, and I felt cheated and deceived. The point is that if you are dishonest with others, they will ultimately figure you out, and when they do, they will have little else to do with you. That is the effect of dishonesty.

The important point I want to make is that the real issue was what the salesperson was thinking when he lied about the first couch being a leather couch. He was thinking about making a sale and was not thinking about being honest! His motive was to get me to buy something, not to give me the best service and treatment he could give me. He was thinking about himself more than his customer, and it cost him the sale when his dishonesty was discovered. I'm sure he was so accustomed to being deceptive that the issue of honesty wasn't even on his radar screen. You need to make sure honesty is a priority in your life!

Character

Sometimes all it takes is a word, a phrase, or a thought planted in someone's mind to change his or her whole life. It truly pays to watch closely what and how you think. Our thinking really does drive our character. Frank Outlaw expressed the power of our thoughts this way:

- *Watch your thoughts; they become words.*
- *Watch your words; they become actions.*
- *Watch your actions; they become habits.*
- *Watch your habits; they become character.*
- *Watch your character; for it becomes your destiny!*

The point I want to make here is that your character truly does become your destiny, because your character determines your future. And your character is largely formed by how you see yourself in relationship to God and other people.

In his beautiful book *Rising Above the Crowd,* Brian Harbour tells the story of Ben Hooper. This story means so much to me I told it in my book *Over the Top,* and I'm going to tell it again here. Ben Hooper was born in the foothills of East Tennessee to an unwed mother. As a result, he and his mother were severely ostracized by their small community. People would say mean things, and the children wouldn't play with Ben at school. American culture has certainly changed since those days, but at the time of Ben Hooper 's birth, being an illegitimate child was scandalous!

When Ben was twelve years old, a new young preacher came to pastor the little church in Ben's town. Almost immediately Ben started hearing exciting things about this preacher, like how loving and nonjudgmental he was, how he accepted people just as they were, and how when he was with someone, he made them feel like the most important person in the world. One Sunday, though he had never been to church a day in his life, Ben Hooper decided he was going to go and hear this preacher. He got there late and he left early because he did not want to attract any attention, but he liked what he heard. For the first time in that young boy's life, he caught just a glimmer of hope. Ben began to get the idea that he could amount to something and that God loved him in spite of his not having a known earthly father.

Ben was back in church the next Sunday—and the next and the next, and his hope grew each Sunday. On about the sixth or seventh Sunday, the message was so moving and exciting that Ben forgot to make his early exit. It was almost as if there was a sign behind the preacher 's head that read, "For you, little Ben Hooper of unknown parentage, there is hope!" When the service was over, Ben suddenly felt a hand on his shoulder. He turned around and looked up, right into the eyes of the young preacher, who asked him a question that had been on the mind of every person there for the last twelve years: "Whose boy are you?" Instantly, the church grew deathly quiet. Then, slowly, a smile started to spread across the face of the young preacher until it broke into a huge grin and he exclaimed, "Oh! I know whose boy you are! Why, the family resemblance is unmistakable. You are a child of God!" And with that the young preacher swatted him across the rear and said, "That's quite an inheritance you've got there, boy! Now, go and see to it that you live up to it." Many, many years later, Ben Hooper said that was the day he was elected and later re-elected governor of the state of Tennessee.

Our character is formed by who we think we are and the standards and principles we embrace in our minds as truth. When Ben Hooper began to see himself as a child of God, he began to see life differently. He had standards to live up to, and his character had to match those standards.

Faith

In 1972, I met an African American woman by the name of Sister Jessie. She was a small woman with big faith, and I invited her to spend the Fourth of July holiday with me and my family. She arrived talking about Jesus and kept it up for three days! Every word she spoke involved praise for her Lord and Savior, Jesus. She spoke of His love and the sacrifice He made on the cross for the sins of the world—which included all of mine! She convinced me that I needed to give my life to Christ, and her words fell on the fertile soil of my heart. I went to bed thinking about all Sister Jessie had said, and that night I became a Christian. I repented of my sin and accepted Jesus as my Savior and the Lord of my life. There were no big fireworks—just a deep, abiding faith that I'd never be the same ol' Zig again. For the first time in my life, I had acquired real faith in something greater than Zig, and I was forever changed. As a matter of fact, at the time of Sister Jessie's visit I was broke, in debt, and needing a miracle. I got one, but it wasn't the kind I thought I needed.

You see, up until Sister Jessie's visit, I had been operating my life, which included my mind and my body, in ways that were not consistent with the owner 's manual! If you buy a lawn mower or a car, you get written instructions about what it takes to make the equipment work best and how to make it last a long time. God's instruction manual (the Holy Bible) does exactly the same thing. If you believe you are a spiritual creature, there are spiritual principles that govern the "equipment" you are attempting to operate.

Before I became a Christian, I was operating my life without an instruction manual, and I was getting the bad results you'd expect.

To me, the issue of faith and living by spiritual principles is just a matter of good common sense. I'm not an animal. I'm like Ben Hooper, a child of God, and I have an inheritance to live up to. So do you. I don't know what you think or believe about spirituality, faith, the Bible, Christianity, or anything else. All I know is that you need to know for yourself what you believe about these issues if you really want to have the kind of success I'm describing to you in *Born to Win*.

Integrity

"Integrity is when you are one with God,
yourself, and your loved ones."
—Dwight "Ike" Reighard

"He who walks with integrity walks securely, but he
who perverts his ways will become known."
—Proverbs 10:9

Integrity has been described as "doing the right thing when nobody is looking." When you try to hide your behavior behind a mask of lies, you live with the constant fear of somebody finding out! All of us know this experience to some degree. Some of us stay on track most of the time and only occasionally fear being found out, but others have lied so much to cover their tracks that they don't remember what's true anymore.

When the Bible talks about our "heart," it is referring to the most inner part of us. Our spiritual heart is a seat of reflection, and it is the place in which we keep our motives and the secret thoughts of our life. Our heart enables us to look at our life clearly, without distortion or embellishment—if our heart is pure and seeks to be obedient to God.

The truth about what is really in our hearts is probably a mixed bag. If we are honest, we have to admit that our motives are not always pure and that we also have big doses of selfishness that take over our lives from time to time. The key to spiritual growth is being able and willing to look into our hearts and be honest about what we find there. Do we find a heart that is focused on spiritual truth, integrity, and honesty? Or do we find something else?

So integrity is a matter of the heart when you get to the bottom of it. Our integrity is a fruit of who and what we are, and we can no more stop our integrity, or lack of it, than an apple tree can stop producing apples and start producing peaches. If you want to know what the status of your own integrity is, just do some serious soul-searching, and that begins by taking a look at your heart, your motives, and the reasons you do everything you do.

Love

There are many different perceptions of what love is and isn't. For most people, love is related to attraction to the opposite sex. But the kind of love I'm talking about is a selfless form of love.

We know we genuinely love when thinking about the needs of others is more fun than thinking about ourselves. There is another thing about love you need to understand. Faking love is impossible.

Love is one of those heart issues we previously discussed, and like the other fruits that we produce in life, it results from who we are. The Bible has the best definition of love you will ever find, and here it is:

Love is patient,
Love is kind.

Love is not jealous,
Love does not brag,
Love is not arrogant.
Love does not act unbecomingly or seek its own;
Love is not provoked and does not take into account a wrong suffered.

—1 Corinthians 13:4-5
New American Standard (SIC)

Loyalty

The final foundation stone is loyalty, and unfortunately it is in short supply these days. Loyalty is one of the characteristics of great leaders, and the reason we have a short supply of inspiring leaders is because we have a short supply of people who have learned how to be loyal. People who are loyal are loyal to the commitments they make, and they keep their promises. They are loyal to the principles they embrace, and they are loyal to the people who fill their lives. A person who is loyal does not talk behind the backs of those he follows, and a loyal person sincerely wishes the best for others. In one sense, loyalty is an expression of love, because it requires some selflessness.

Few people have become great leaders without first learning how to be loyal. If a person holds a position of leadership and responsibility, his effectiveness will be directly related to how well he learned in his formative years to follow others and to be loyal to them. A person without loyalty will not follow others and is incapable of being an effective leader.

Now you understand why you have to be before you can *do*, and *do* before you can *have. Be, do, have* is a picture of the whole person, inside and out. You become what you are because it is impossible to produce results that are inconsistent with who you are. As you begin to plan your vision and your goals, this truth needs to be an integral, foundational aspect of your character. Then, and only then, can you begin to develop the degree of clarity, the topic of the next chapter, that you need to keep moving toward the life you are meant to have.

CHAPTER THREE

KNOW WHAT YOU WANT

In chapter 1, we covered that you must want to win. In chapter 2, we boldly presented the case that you must build a solid foundation to begin the winning process. Now it's time to get clear about exactly what you want. Clarity will increase your desire and move you in the direction of your goals and dreams. America's foremost business philosopher Jim Rohn said, "It's not the direction of the wind, but the setting of the sails that really matters."

I want to remind you that you were *born to win*, but to be the winner you were born to be, you have to have a clear plan to get there. This means having specific goals that you are shooting for.

I once heard of a book called *I'd Rather Eat Nails than Set Goals*. I never read the book, but I certainly understand the sentiment. Goals make us accountable, and lots of people avoid setting them for that reason. There are many good reasons for becoming a goal setter, and here are just a few of them.

SIX REASONS TO SET GOALS

1. Goals bring the future into the present, and the present is the only time we can take action. Setting goals makes it possible to do something today to create the future you want.

2. If you don't plan your time, someone else will help you waste it.
3. People get twice as much done on the day before they go on vacation, because they plan (set goals) and prioritize what they intend to do. Thought: if you lived every day like it was the day before vacation, how much would you be able to increase the total productivity of your life?
4. Goal setters make more money than people who don't set goals. When Dave Jensen was the Chief Administrative Officer at UCLA in 1992, he conducted a study on goal setting. He learned that people with a balanced goals program earned an average of $7,411 per month. In 2011, those numbers showed earnings of $11,632.73 per month. Dave discovered that individuals without a goals program earned an average of $3,397 per month, or $5,332.13 in 2011 dollars and cents. That's over $6,000 more a month! Those with goals programs were also happier and healthier and got along better with the folks at home.
5. Goals keep you focused on the things that really matter and help you avoid wasting time on things that are unproductive. Focus helps you change from being a "wandering generality" to being a "meaningful specific."
6. Setting goals gives direction and purpose to all that you do. Goals are the links in the chain that connect activity to accomplishment.

NO MORE EXCUSES

People make a lot of excuses for not being willing to set goals, but the benefits of setting goals far exceed the excuses for not setting them. There is something about the

IT IS BETTER TO SET GOALS AND HAVE DIRECTION THAN TO NOT HAVE GOALS AND WANDER AROUND IN CONFUSION.

goal-setting process that makes people approach it in fear, and they can find lots and lots of reasons to avoid it. The biggest reason is an unwillingness to be accountable for results. After all, if you set a goal and fail to reach it, some people will consider it failure. But there is an old saying that goes, "It is better to have tried and failed than not to have tried at all!" I would alter that concept slightly and say, *It is better to set goals and have direction than to not have goals and wander around in confusion*. Ultimately, people who do not set goals are just making up their life as they go along, which results in unreached potential.

Born to Win is a journey, and every journey has a beginning. When I say you are *born to win*, I'm talking about your entire life, not just a piece of it. Remember the Wheel of Life I mentioned previously? It is a powerful tool to help you begin your *Born to Win* journey, and I encourage you to make use of it. Before you can prepare to change your life you must have an accurate picture of what your life is like now—and it must be an honest picture. Remember that honesty is one of the foundation stones for success, and it begins with being honest about yourself! Unfortunately, people have an uncanny ability to inflate their good qualities and deflate their deficiencies. If you do that in the Wheel of Life exercise, you will get a distorted picture of your starting point that will impact how well you are able to hit the goals and targets you plan to achieve.

A VISUAL STARTING PLACE FOR GOAL SETTING—THE WHEEL OF LIFE

Take a look at the following graphic and then do the simple exercise I suggest.

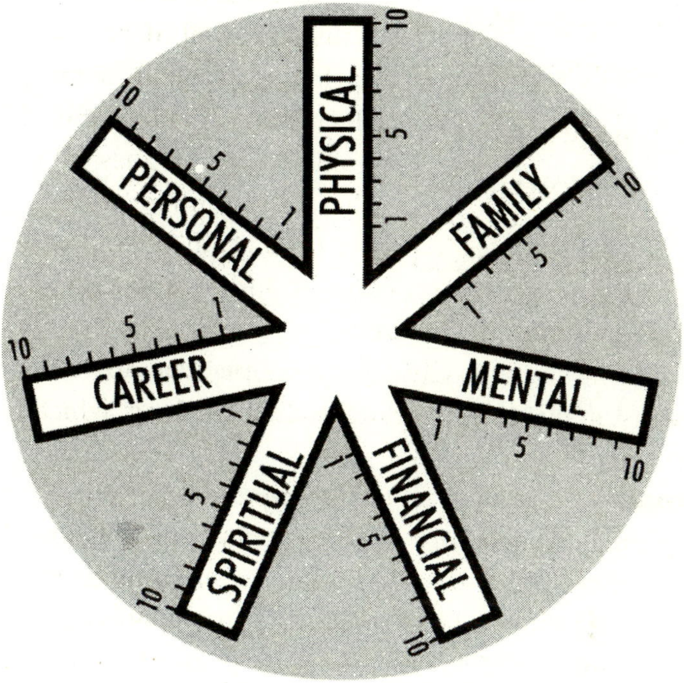

Read each of the category lists carefully and rate yourself on a scale of 1-10 in each space. Rate yourself with 1 being very poor and 10 being outstanding. For example, under Physical rate your own appearance. Do you look fit and well kept? Do this for all of the categories. You may have done this before. That's OK, you need to do it again and again – and every six months for the rest of your life. Now add up the total of each column and divide that number by 10. This will give you your personal score for that particular spoke on the wheel. Now go ahead and mark that number on your spoke, and mark the rest of the spokes. Now connect the dots. What does your Wheel of Life look like? Is it round? Do you have flat spots? Do you have several spokes that need improvement?

Physical

______ appearance
______ regular checkup
______ energy level
______ muscles toned
______ regular fitness program
______ weight control
______ diet & nutrition
______ stress control
______ endurance & strength
______ other ____________
______ TOTAL ÷ 10 = _____

Mental

______ attitude
______ intelligence
______ formal education
______ continuing education & training
______ creative imagination
______ inspirational reading
______ compact disc education
______ inquisitive mind
______ self-image
______ enthusiasm
______ other ____________
______ TOTAL ÷ 10 = ______

Spiritual

______ believe in God
______ inner peace
______ influence on others
______ spouse relationship
______ church involvement
______ sense of purpose
______ attitude for giving donations
______ prayer
______ Bible study
______ other ____________
______ TOTAL ÷ 10 =

Family

______ listening
______ good role model
______ principled but flexible
______ forgiving attitude
______ build self-esteem of others
______ express love and respect
______ meals together
______ family relationships
______ dealing with disagreements
______ time together
______ other ____________
______ TOTAL ÷ 10 = ______

Financial

______ proper priority
______ personal budget
______ impulse purchases
______ earnings
______ living within income
______ charge accounts kept current
______ adequate insurance
______ investments
______ financial statement
______ other ____________
______ TOTAL ÷ 10 = ____

Personal

______ recreation
______ exercise
______ friendships
______ community activities
______ service clubs
______ quiet time
______ growth time
______ consistent life
______ other ______________
______ TOTAL ÷ 10 = ______

Career

______ like what I do
______ understand my job
______ co-worker relationships
______ productivity
______ understand company goals
______ understand my activity in relationship to my goals
______ appreciate company benefits
______ opportunity for advancement
______ career transition
______ well-trained for my job
______ other ___________________
______ TOTAL ÷ 10 = ___________

Let me ask you a question – how smooth is your ride? If your wheel has flat spots, or it's a small wheel, that means your ride is pretty bumpy and you are really not going anywhere. Now that you know where you are, you have a place to begin when you start setting goals.

If you will make it a practice to follow the steps in this chapter, it will separate you from the rest of the pack. It will give you the winning edge and move you constantly in the direction of the dreams you desire.

Once again, knowing where you are is an important part in the *Born to Win* philosophy and is absolutely essential to getting where you want to go. When you complete this exercise, you will clearly see where your life is today and the specific areas you need to address to set powerful and effective goals that will place your feet on the path of your *Born to Win* journey.

Were you surprised by the results of this exercise? Most people are a little shocked to see that their wheel is lopsided with some flat spots, rather than a nice round wheel that permits them to roll successfully through life. Perhaps you have a fairly round wheel but everything is a 2 or 3. Your ride may be smooth, but you are not going anywhere. The *Born to Win* concept will help you remove the flat spots and produce a wheel full of conditions that approach or become 10s. It begins with planning your future around the seven spokes of the wheel and setting the right goals to achieve the vision you have for yourself.

KNOW WHERE YOU'RE GOING

A young couple, lost on a rural road, spotted an old farmer, so they stopped the car and asked him a question. "Sir, could you tell us where this road will take us?" Without a moment's hesitation the old farmer said, "Son, this road will take you anywhere in the world you want to go, if you are moving in the right direction." This little story makes a big point. From wherever you are, you can go anywhere you want to go if you pick the right roads to travel. The roads you travel in life are selected and determined by the goals you set for each area of your life. The key is to pick the right roads!

Now you might be thinking, "Zig, how do I know what goals to set, and how do I know they are the right goals that will put me on the roads I need to travel to get where I want to go?" Well, I'm glad you asked, because I most certainly plan to tell you! I have a proven seven-step process you can apply to your goal setting, and if you follow each step correctly, you will create goals that are tailor-made for you and what you want to achieve. I've been teaching this process for my entire career, and the proof of its effectiveness is in the lives of the people who have followed my advice and done it! Before we get started, I want to clearly say that you must do the seven steps for *each* goal that you set. You will want to set multiple goals for each spoke in the Wheel of Life, and you will apply this seven-step process to each goal.

THE SEVEN STEPS OF GOAL SETTING

1. Identify the goal

If you don't identify a target, you will never hit it. When you identify a goal, it means that you write it down and describe it clearly. Don't set any nebulous targets. If you want to have specific success, you must have specific targets. A goal "to increase my annual income" or "to spend more time on my spiritual life" is not specific. A specific goal would be "to increase my current income by 20 percent" or "to read the entire Bible from cover to maps."

2. List the benefits: what's in it for me?

Once you identify a specific goal, you need to list the benefits you will receive when you reach that goal. Let's face it, we only do the things we want to do and are willing to do. If there are no personal benefits, your motivation for completing the goal will be diminished. Remember that changing your life is not always easy, and you will hit some rough spots in the road as you move forward. You will need all the personal motivation you can muster, and understanding what's in it for you is vitally important. Don't skimp on this step!

3. List the obstacles to overcome

I believe I just mentioned that there might be some rough spots on your journey as you work to achieve your goals. Many of them can be anticipated, and if you can anticipate something, you can prepare yourself in advance to overcome it. So think it through and make a complete list of all the things that can prevent you from being successful. Ask a trusted friend who knows you well to help you finish the list.

4. List the skills and knowledge required

Knowledge gives us the power to accomplish things we would not otherwise be able to do, and skills give us the tools to take advantage of our knowledge. There is a direct relationship between knowing and doing, and successfully accomplishing your goals will require that powerful combination. For example, if your goal is to increase your proficiency on the computer, you will need to know specifically what the computer can do for you (knowledge). Once you know what you want the computer to do for you, the skills you will need to be successful must be identified. The skills might include learning to type on a keyboard with two hands instead of finger pecking. This would trigger setting another goal of learning to type! Never forget that knowledge and skill will be required to successfully complete any goal.

5. Identify the people and groups to work with

We do a better job when we have the help of others. They can help us with knowledge and skill and can offer valuable advice we need to be successful. So when you set your goals, always consider the people and the groups you can work with that can help you be more successful.

6. Develop a plan of action

This is the most critical step, and it involves thinking through the details of how you will achieve your goal. In my younger years I was thirty-seven pounds overweight. I had put that weight on one bite at a time, and I was going to have to lose it the same way. That required a plan! I wanted to lose my weight over a ten-month period and that was the first step of the plan. Thirty-seven pounds sounds like a lot, but when you realize it's only 3.7 pounds a month over a ten-month period it sounds a lot better. So, I planned to lose 3.7 pounds a month for ten months. Then I included a daily running and exercise plan in the goal, as well as a diet that would limit my caloric intake. With those details planned, I clearly knew how I was going to have to live each day to be successful. I prepared diligently to succeed. I stuck to my plan (which means I never made the first exception), and ten months later I had lost thirty-seven pounds. Success would have eluded me had I not planned the details of what I would do each day to reach my goal. In this case, reaching my goal may not have changed *the* world but it surely did change *my* world.

7. Set a deadline for achievement

In the example above, you notice I gave myself ten months to lose the weight I wanted to lose. I had a great reason for setting that deadline—I believe in goal setting, and all goals need a completion date to be effective. I was in the process of writing my first book, *See You At the Top,* and I had ten months left to complete my book by my goal date when it struck me that I was not a good example of the very things I was teaching. Nobody who saw me was going to believe a word I said, because I was not taking care of the health portion of my life. There was no way an overweight fat boy could effectively tell other people how to change their lives without first changing his own! My integrity was on the line... so I sought help at Dr. Kenneth Cooper's Aerobics Center, where Dr. Randy Martin told me the true state of my condition. With his help, I made my ten-month plan.

If you don't set a deadline for completing your goals, you will not be accountable to yourself or anyone else. If you are not accountable for your goals, you will not achieve them.

WHEN YOU "PAY THE PRICE"—YOU ENJOY THE BENEFITS

Some goals require personal sacrifice and a lot of dedication and effort to achieve. When I was in the process of losing my weight, it was hard to discipline myself to run and exercise each day, regardless of the weather or how I felt. It was hard to resist eating all the things I thought about. In many ways, I felt like a bit of a martyr, denying myself the pleasures in which others could so freely indulge. I was "paying the price" of achieving my goal.

When I was fifty years old, I was speaking in Portland, Oregon, and I went for my daily jog at the Portland State University track. As I ran around the track I saw lots of young students moving about the campus. It suddenly occurred to me that, at age fifty, I was in better shape than 95 percent of those students. I knew I could outrun just about all of them over a two-mile course. That is when it became obvious—I was enjoying the benefits of achieving my weight-loss goal.

The point is that the successful completion of a goal will produce specific, tangible benefits that will last a long time! Do you remember Step 2 in the goal-setting process? Identify the benefits and identify what's in it for you. That is a critical step, and that's why you need to identify lots of benefits so you can stay motivated to maintain the discipline you will need to do the daily things you have to do to achieve your goal. I pursue my goals because of the benefits I will receive from doing them. You can do the same.

GOAL SETTING IS ABOUT *BECOMING*

I want to be certain you have the right attitude about setting your goals. Don't think of goal setting as a tire-some activity that requires you to do things that are difficult. The real benefit of having goals is what you become by reaching them. When you successfully complete your goals, you change specific things in your life. Take a look at the Wheel of Life and think about the new person you will be if you can become or approach being a 10 in every spoke of the wheel. I can tell you factually that your life will be radically changed for the better, and the person you become will be highly successful in all that you do.

Are you convinced that you need to become a goal setter? Have you started thinking about where you are and where you would like to be? Have you started listing the obstacles that stand between you and success? I hope you are sufficiently motivated to begin the goal-setting process, because goals represent the action tools you need to be able to plan to win. Do you remember when I said you have to *be* before you can *do*, and you have to *do* before you can *have*? Being a successful goal setter is the process that enables you to be the person you need to *be*, by *doing* what you have to do, so you can change yourself and the world for the better.

CHAPTER FOUR

VALUE AND PURPOSE: THE DRIVING FORCES THAT FUEL ACTION

So far, we have considered who you are and what you do. Now we're going to examine the why. When we know why we're doing something, when we have a clear understanding of the value of our actions and the purpose for those actions, it's easier to stay motivated even when our energy is flagging. The "why" in life is your value and purpose. When you've got a strong enough why, you can always find the how.

Part of planning to win is developing the fuel that will drive you to take the daily actions that will move you in the direction of your dreams. When you skimp on planning, the results you get in the end will be reduced. In this chapter I'm going to disclose what it takes to sustain your efforts so that you will turn your vision and your dream into reality. The fact is that diminished effort will produce diminished results, and it's human nature to let down a little the longer we do something.

Have you ever noticed that sports contests are frequently won or lost in the final minutes of a game? One competitor outlasts and outplays their opponent in the final minutes and is able to execute more effectively and move on to victory. Success in life is much the same. You have to have a plan, and you have to execute that plan consistently—even when you don't feel like it. Vince Lombardi said that "winning is not a sometime thing... it's an all the time thing."

> IF YOU WANT TO BECOME THE WINNER YOU WERE BORN TO BE, IT'S GOING TO TAKE CHANGING YOUR DAILY ACTIONS UNTIL THEY BECOME A HABIT.

If you want to become the winner you were born to be, it's going to take changing your daily actions until they become a habit.

Understanding the power of value and purpose and how to use it for lasting motivation is essential to maintaining your intensity level so you will consistently do what you need to do to gain and maintain a winning edge. The *Born to Win* process is about being the best you can be, and to be the best you can be, you must commit yourself to taking the necessary daily actions required to make that happen. This means understanding the reasons behind the vision. Why do you want this plan? If you win, what will it accomplish, who will it help? How will you feel? How will this vision and plan value others? How will it add value to your life? When you understand those principles and the work you need to do to build your plan around those principles, the result will be contentment, happiness, and a mental perspective that will enable you to approach life in a more enthusiastic and effective way. The fact that you have created a vision and understand the true value and purpose of that vision will energize you and give you the personal motivation you need to finish well—and achieve exceptional results.

COOKED IN THE SQUAT

When I was growing up, one of our neighbors had a cook, and I had occasion to enjoy her cooking every now and then. One day when I was there, the cook pulled a pan of biscuits out of the oven, and they weren't much thicker than a silver dollar. I asked her what happened to make those biscuits so skinny. She said, "Sweetheart, those biscuits squatted to rise, but they just got cooked in the squat!"

When you make bread, the dough starts out kind of flat; eventually, the yeast in the dough will make it rise. If you cook the dough before it has completely risen, it will get "cooked in the squat." If you think of the squatting time for bread as being the same as the planning process for success, you will see how this can be a valuable lesson. If you don't take the time to plan properly (and this includes knowing the purpose and value of what you are working for), chances are you will get cooked in the squat and will never "rise" to your full potential.

Most people have heard of Mahatma Gandhi, the man who led India to independence from British rule. His life has been memorialized in books and film, and he is regarded as one of the great men in history. But did you know Gandhi did not start out as a great hero? He was born into a middle-class family. He had low self-esteem, and that made him reluctant to interact with others. He wasn't a very good student, either, and he struggled just to finish high school. His first attempt at higher education ended in five months. His parents decided to send him to England to finish his education, hoping the new environment would motivate him. Gandhi became a lawyer. The problem when he returned to India was that he didn't know much about Indian law and had trouble finding clients. So he migrated to South Africa and got a job as a clerk. Gandhi's life changed one day while riding on a train in South Africa in the first-class section. Because of his dark skin, he was forced to move to a freight car. He refused, and they kicked him off the train. It was then he realized he was afraid of challenging authority, but that he suddenly wanted to help others overcome discrimination if he could. He created a new vision for himself that had value and purpose. He saw value in helping people free themselves from discrimination and injustice. He discovered purpose in life where none had existed previously, and that sense of purpose pulled him forward and motivated him to do what best-selling author and motivational speaker Andy Andrews calls "persist without exception." His purpose and value turned him into the winner he was born to be, and Gandhi became one of the greatest men of history.

Without that new vision and purpose, the chances are pretty good that Gandhi would have remained a struggling lawyer/clerk and nobody would have heard of him. He would have been "cooked in the squat"! But Gandhi was not cooked in the squat because he developed a sense of value and purpose for his life, and based on that, he was able to set specific goals to turn his vision into reality! He eventually led an entire nation to independence without firing a shot!

ANYONE WITH A PURPOSE CAN MAKE A DIFFERENCE

Most people are not destined to be as famous as Gandhi, but everyday people living everyday lives often find themselves at a crossroad where the inward focus of their life becomes others-centered. Once their purpose is defined, their value increases.

This was the case with Mary A. Michel, CEO and founder of Journey of the Heart Ministries. Mary's personal experience of overcoming multiple losses gave her a heart of compassion for suffering women, and in August of 1998, her vision for Journey of the Heart and the Centers of Hope was born.

Mary's passion drove her to leave her professional business career and get the training she needed to make her vision a reality. Over the years Mary has been privileged and honored to personally mentor more than one hundred women and, through her experience and training, now offers this leadership to Journey of the Heart, the Center of Hope volunteers, and the community. With a reputation for having a positive approach to difficult situations, Mary Michel gives women hope and helps them discover a victorious life. Her purpose is well defined, and her value increases with each woman who finds a better way to live and a better life. For more information about Mary and Journey of the Heart, please visit www.journeyoftheheart.org.

HAVING VALUE AND PURPOSE CAN UNLOCK YOUR POTENTIAL

The idea of value and purpose is linked to the concept of discovering a greater good, a mission, or a higher calling. Some people find their value and purpose in their spiritual faith. I am one of those. Before I became a Christian at age forty-five, I was firmly entrenched in acceptable mediocrity.

By that I mean I was doing some good things and was impacting a number of people's lives, but in truth I was broke and in debt. I had a general vision about what I wanted, but the depth of value and purpose was missing. I was doing things because I wanted to do them, and I wanted the results to be for me. After I accepted Christ, I suddenly had a higher purpose and new values. I wanted to help others be all they could be, and I wanted it solely for their happiness and peace—not mine. You might say ol' Zig became "others-centered" rather than "self-centered."

When that new sense of value and purpose took over my mind and my heart, I began to have success beyond my wildest dreams. I think I felt much the way Gandhi felt when they kicked him off the train. I could now see that my efforts up to that point had been based on the wrong things and why the results I was getting were less than spectacular. When I changed my focus, I changed my motives, and that is when I began my "new career."

Shortly after that conversion experience I wrote my signature book, *See You at the Top*, and I haven't had to solicit a speaking engagement since. For the past forty years my vision of wanting to be a difference-maker and an encourager in the lives of others, and to help people reach their full potential, has pulled me forward with a laser-like focus. I never forget the value and purpose of what I do, and that is what keeps me going... I love what I do.

UNDERSTANDING VALUE AND PURPOSE

Value and purpose are about understanding the specific benefits you will help people receive if they receive what you have for them. Three men were busy at the same task, and a passerby stopped and asked each of the men what they were doing. The first man said, "I am cutting stone." The second man said, "I am earning my living." The third man said, "I am building a cathedral." All three of the men were involved in cutting stone. The first man saw no purpose or value in what he was doing, and my guess is that his days were long and tedious. He probably went home tired and exhausted every night and dreaded going to work each day. The second man had a different perspective. He saw cutting the stones as a means to earn a living and probably had a better attitude than the first man. However, the value and purpose he saw in his effort was merely about getting his paycheck. I imagine this man spent a lot of time thinking about other jobs he might be able to get and probably found his work boring and repetitive.

The third man knew he was cutting stone, and he knew he was earning a paycheck, but he also saw value and purpose in his work that transcended those basic realities. The third man was building a cathedral that would be used by people. The cathedral would be a spiritual and social center where men and women could come to worship and fellowship together. That church, when completed, would give people hope and help them live better lives. What do you think the third man's attitude was about his work? My guess is that he couldn't wait to get to work every day. I imagine he arrived early and stayed late. He probably talked about his work all the time and was grateful to be doing something that was so much fun! I'm sure he could visualize that finished church in his mind and couldn't wait to go there.

Do you see how understanding value and purpose can make the difference in how we approach our lives and our work? It's absolutely critical to reaching your full potential and avoiding being "cooked in the squat."

FINDING YOUR WHY

I SUGGEST THAT YOU ASK YOURSELF THE FOLLOWING BIG QUESTION SO THAT THE VALUE AND PURPOSE OF YOUR VISION WILL BE CLEARLY UNDERSTOOD.

Understanding the value and purpose of something requires that you pursue the "why" questions related to your vision. In the last chapter I gave you a seven-step process that essentially walked you through the "why" questions for each of your goals. Goals are little "mini-visions" that, when assembled as a total program within your Wheel of Life, will turn your vision into reality. But you also need to ask another set of "why" questions about your overall vision, as well. When you have stated your vision in clear terms, I suggest that you ask yourself the following *big* question so that the value and purpose of your vision will be clearly understood.

Here it is: why did *you* create *your* vision? Think about it: why did you create your vision? What was your motivating force for creating your vision in the first place? Is it something you really want, or is it something you think you "should" want? Is your motivation characterized by what you can get, versus what you can give? Did you create your vision based on the needs of others and out of a sincere belief that you can help those people get what they want? Or did you come up with your vision just to make more money? Don't get me wrong. I have absolutely nothing against making money. I've been broke and I've been flush, and I can tell you it's a lot more fun to be flush. The undeniable fact, however, is that I made a lot more money after I began to focus on really helping other people get what they want.

The answers to these "why" questions will reveal if your vision is self-centered or others-centered. You recall that I mentioned that my own life changed when my vision and my goals became others-centered. If your vision is mostly self-centered, it will have diminished value, and the purpose of it will be questionable. Remember, *you can have everything in life you want if you will just help enough other people get what they want*. That statement captures a principle that is others-centered. It is not a self-centered strategy! But it is a strategy

YOU CAN HAVE EVERYTHING IN LIFE YOU WANT IF YOU WILL JUST HELP ENOUGH OTHER PEOPLE GET WHAT THEY WANT.

that, when followed, will change your life and the lives of many others along the way.

I am closing this chapter with a special story about a mother who knows her purpose and the value of her life-changing, life-giving efforts. Sandy Sides has an easy answer for the "why" question: "Savannah!"

Savannah Sides was only five years old when she and her mother were in a head-on automobile accident. Sandy was seriously injured, and Savannah died of a massive brain injury within hours of the accident. When told that Savannah had no brain function, her father remembered his little girl's request to be an organ donor and asked the doctor to make the arrangements. Savannah's spontaneous and selfless decision brought some good out of the tragedy of that day, and at least four lives were changed for the better.

In spite of having more than twenty surgeries, having to learn how to walk again, and living with constant side effects of the accident, Sandy hosts an annual motorcycle ride called the "Savannah Faith Miracle Ride." She does it for two reasons. First, she wants to honor her daughter's memory, and second, she wants to continue her daughter's legacy of organ donation by raising funds to help organ transplant candidates.

Sandy Sides is making a difference because she is passionate about her purpose, and I believe the value of what she is doing exceeds calculation! For more information about Sandy and the annual ride, please visit www.savannahmr.org.

Part Two

Preparing to Win

CHAPTER FIVE

YOU CAN DO MORE THAN YOU THINK

Your experience influences how high you think you can go. Preparing yourself to win is crucial to success. I once heard that preparation is the foundation for any level of achievement. I am totally convinced this is so. Whether you are preparing for an athletic event, an important speech, a sales call, or a camping trip, the better prepared you are, the better the results. The great Tom Landry said, "If you are prepared, you will be confident... and you will do the job." It's true: planning and preparing gives you the confidence you need and the right to expect to win.

What does it mean to be prepared? It means equipping yourself with the tools, skills, knowledge, and attitude you will need to achieve all that you planned. I hope you set lots of high goals for yourself after reading part 1 of *Born to Win*. I know the completion of those goals will lead you to the successful attainment of your vision. But what if your vision is to become a jet pilot, and you don't know how to fly? I think you get the idea. To become a jet pilot you will have a lot of preparation and equipping to do before you have a shot at turning your vision into reality. So, as we begin this second stage of the *Born to Win* process, whenever

I say *prepare*, just understand I'm talking about equipping yourself with the tools, skills, knowledge, and attitudes you need to turn your plans into reality.

One of my favorite stories is about flea training. I'm going to tell it again here because it is the perfect illustration of how your experience can limit what you are able to accomplish. If you put a bunch of fleas in a jar and put a lid on the jar, the fleas will jump up and collide with the jar lid. They quickly adjust how high they jump so they won't hit the lid. After they adjust their jumping power to avoid the lid, you can take the lid off of the jar and the fleas will not jump out! They will have trained themselves to jump so high and no higher. The fleas actually become slaves to their experience and imprison themselves inside the jar—even though they could jump out at any time after the lid is removed.

People do the same thing to themselves. Somewhere in most people's experience, they develop the idea that they can (or should) do only so much and no more. They adjust their expectations of themselves accordingly, and they get what they expect: less than what they are capable of!

I believe you have the potential to do and accomplish far more than you believe you are capable of doing and accomplishing! I believe that because history is filled with stories of men and women who have done just that. If you study the lives of great people, you usually discover they came from average families, living average lives, doing very average things. Then, these people have some kind of experience or encounter a turning point that puts them in position to do more than they could even conceive. Or possibly they became sick and tired of living the way they were living and finally said, "Enough is enough!" In every instance they responded to the experience or opportunity and accepted the challenge to grow.

Former United States President Dwight Eisenhower was not a high-ranking officer in the years prior to World War II, but he was passionate about wanting to get out from behind a desk and fight "his war." He was a staff officer to General Douglas MacArthur in the Philippines prior to the war and probably thought continuing in that role would be the best thing he could do. Circumstances of the war and his excellent organizational skills eventually resulted in him becoming the Supreme Commander of all the Allied Armies in Europe, and after the war he was elected president of the United States. Eisenhower is actually quoted as saying, *"I thought it completely absurd to mention my name in the same breath as the presidency."*

The amazing and even startling point of this story is that there was never one *big* thing Eisenhower did that changed the course of his life. Every small step, every small promotion, every new direction his military life took led to a culmination of events that resulted in his huge lifetime of success. His willingness to accept every new position, regardless of how mundane or challenging it might be, moved Dwight Eisenhower toward his destiny.

ARE YOU WILLING TO TAKE A RISK?

One of the main reasons people fail to reach their full potential is because they are unwilling to risk anything. They are fearful of losing, failing, or getting hurt and just want to do the things they believe will keep them safe. They simply want to maintain their status quo and avoid anything that might upset the mediocre expectations they have for their lives. Now, I don't want you to get the idea that I am making fun of people who have mediocre expectations. Most people have mediocre expectations for themselves, and they come by it naturally. Their experience has conditioned them to believe mediocrity is about as good as it gets, so their expectations match their experience.

What I'm saying is that experience is a great teacher but we should never let our experience influence what we think about our potential. Did you know that every human being is created with a purpose and that they have a responsibility to not only discover their purpose but also to fulfill it? I don't mean that it is every person's destiny to be rich and famous, but it is every person's destiny to do something that will make a positive difference in the lives of others. That is one of the reasons I believe *you can have everything in life you want if you will just help enough other people get what they want*. I love what Joan of Arc said when she stated, "I'm not afraid. I was born to do this." If you believe as I do that you were *born to win*, you're going to have to find your fears and start facing them. Face them over and over again until you have nothing to fear but fear itself.

> WHAT I'M SAYING IS THAT EXPERIENCE IS A GREAT TEACHER BUT WE SHOULD NEVER LET OUR EXPERIENCE INFLUENCE WHAT WE THINK ABOUT OUR POTENTIAL.

> THE WAY TO CORRECT THIS THINKING IS TO REALIZE THAT THE MISTAKES WE MADE IN OUR PAST ARE ACTUALLY ASSETS THAT WE CAN USE FOR OUR BENEFIT TODAY.

RISK-TAKING

To discover your purpose and act on it, you will have to take risks. What does it mean to take a risk, and how can you overcome the fear of taking risks? First, let's consider how you might have become fearful of taking risks in the first place. Most people become fearful because they have been hurt by taking risks in the past. That is why our experience contributes to possibly limiting what we think we can do or are willing to do. The way to correct this thinking is to realize that the mistakes we made in our past are actually assets that we can use for our benefit today. It is not that we should stop taking risks. It is that we should not repeat things we have done in the past that did not work. There is a big difference between the two!

POSITIVE AND NEGATIVE CHOICES

Now we come to the real issues regarding risk-taking. As I said before, it is not risk-taking that is the problem—it is the tendency we may have to make bad choices. I am sure you have known many people who make the same bad choices over and over again. They almost seem to be in a never-ending downward spiral of bad decision-making. As a result, their lives are a mess. When we make poor choices, our circumstances become worse. As our circumstances become worse, our choices become more limited. As our choices become more limited, the likelihood of making more bad choices is inevitable. On the other hand, when we make good choices, our circumstances improve. As our circumstances improve, we have better opportunities, and better opportunities make it possible for everything in our lives to become better.

Once we begin to make certain types of choices, the likelihood of making similar choices in the future almost becomes a self-fulfilling destiny.

Every time we make a choice, it is either positive or negative. For example, you have the choice to either smoke cigarettes or refuse to smoke cigarettes. If you choose not to smoke cigarettes, that is a positive choice. Making that positive choice immediately produces better health and longer life. You will also smell better and save lots of money.

By making the positive choice to refrain from smoking, the subsequent choices that come to you as a result of that decision are more positive. We can choose to be more active, and we can choose to sit in the part of the restaurant that has clean air. On the other hand, if you choose to smoke cigarettes, your choices begin to move down a more negative path. You will have to decide on filters or non-filters. Will you smoke openly or hide it? What brands of cologne and breath fresheners will you have to buy to mask the odor? Will you choose to have chemo and radiation or surgery—or both? Finally, the last choice will be for a metal or wooden coffin! Of course, someone might have to make that choice for you.

If the fear of attempting to do more than you think you can do is a problem for you, let me ask you a couple of questions. Are you afraid to set goals because you are afraid you might not be able to complete them? Are you afraid of failing in front of friends and family? Is that what keeps you from making a commitment to try something new or stretch yourself? I am a firm believer that goals and commitments should be put in writing, but many people avoid doing that. Somehow, by not putting their goals on paper, they believe they have a built-in explanation for failure. They can say they did not really fail, because they never had the goal in the first place. I hope this is not your approach to goal setting! If it is, it may be safer emotionally and even appear to be a no-risk approach. However, it is also a guarantee that you will never achieve a fraction of your true potential.

Playing it safe by refusing to take risks may seem to be a prudent choice. However, let me point out that it would be safer for ships to stay in the harbor and for airplanes to stay on the ground. By not going to sea or taking to the air, they would be able to avoid the challenges of bad weather and unexpected conditions. But idle ships grow barnacles faster, and idle planes quickly begin to rust. Yes, there is danger in setting goals, but the risk is infinitely greater when you don't set goals. The reason is simple. Just as ships are built to sail the seas and planes to fly the heavens, so is man created for a purpose. That purpose is to get everything out of you that is humanly possible so you can make your contributions to mankind. Winston Churchill said, "Play the game for more than you can afford to lose... only then will you learn the game." John Sculley, past president of Apple, stated, "People who take risks are the people you'll lose against." The bottom line is this: the greatest risk is to never take a risk, therefore dooming yourself to a life of mediocrity. On the other hand, if you take a risk and you fail, what you learn in the process will help you use better judgment in the future.

CHOOSE YOUR FRIENDS AND ASSOCIATES WISELY

Finally, a determining factor that limits our potential and keeps us from being all we can be is the opinions of other people. It is sad to say but there are many negative people in this world who are not successful, and they would prefer that nobody else be successful, either. Has there ever been a time in your life when you shared a dream with one or more people and they turned on you like a pack of wolves? After hearing your dream they all began to tell you why it was impossible and list all the reasons and obstacles that stood in your way. Sadly, there are families that behave this way toward their own flesh and blood. Parents, brothers, and sisters tell their children and siblings all the things they *don't believe they can do*. Sometimes it seems the only advice and support these people can offer guarantees failure. They might as well be saying, "You're not good enough to do what you think you want to do. Who do you think you are, dreaming that kind of dream?" If you have people like this in your life, my advice is to keep your goals to yourself when you are around them. You do not want to become what I call a SNIOP. A SNIOP is a person who is Susceptible to the Negative Influence of Other People. A SNIOP is a person who is more concerned with pleasing people than living their life to its full potential. In other words, a SNIOP lets other people's opinions control and limit their success.

As we talk about preparing ourselves to win, a big part of that preparation is surrounding ourselves with people who are encouragers. While it is true that there are many negative people who take every opportunity to encourage failure, there are others who can help you be successful.

Encouragers are people who have been successful themselves. They are people who stepped up and took risks and were able to accomplish things they may not have believed possible.

Encouragers are the kind of people you can share your goals with and they will encourage you to go for it. Encouragers will also share their own mistakes with you and tell you how they overcame them to achieve success.

My youngest daughter is Julie Ziglar Norman. She is one of the greatest encouragers I have ever known, and I am so proud she is my daughter. Julie is also the editor of many of my books, and she traveled and appeared on stage with me for several years when I spoke using the interview format. Julie and her husband, Jim, faced a crisis in their marriage about fifteen years ago and decided to separate. They went to counseling and worked very hard to rejuvenate and restore their relationship. They were successful, and in 2011 they celebrated their twenty-eighth wedding anniversary. Their four children and twelve grandchildren are the beneficiaries of their success. Julie and Jim both believe that bad marriages can be saved if the couple is willing to do what they have to do to be successful.

During the time of their separation, Julie shared with me the lack of encouragement she got from many of her friends.

Many of them seemed happy she was separated and told her she might as well just get a divorce and find somebody else. Thank goodness she did not take their advice! Today, when Julie has a friend who is having marital difficulty, she immediately begins to encourage them to try to solve their problems. She and Jim both share their experience freely with other people so they can know there are options that are better than divorce. Julie told me that her friends who have marital difficulty remark that she is the only person in their life encouraging them to stay married. It is a sad reality that a couple experiencing difficulty will get more advice to end their marriage than encouragement to fix it. Surround yourself with people who want the best for you and the people you love!

GO FOR IT!

There's more in store for you in your life than you can possibly imagine. I promise you it is the truth. To reach your full potential, you have to set goals that will stretch you. You must not be afraid of taking risks. You must learn to recognize opportunities and have the courage to pursue them. You have to make better choices that will provide better results. Finally, you need to avoid the negative influences of other people and surround yourself with successful people who will encourage you to pursue your dreams.

CHAPTER SIX
KNOWLEDGE GIVES YOU POWER

A simple fact about success is that it requires a lot of positive, personal motivation to achieve. The motivation is required to get you through the difficulties and struggles that happen along the way. You can be sure that in any effort there will be unexpected, seemingly big setbacks on your journey. Many times these unexpected circumstances can be so discouraging you might even be tempted to give up on your goal or vision.

In my book *Embrace the Struggle* I state, "Getting knocked down in life is a given; getting up and moving forward is a choice." That's where knowledge comes in. Applied knowledge gives you the power to see past today's challenges. This is why you have to feed your mind with the good, the clean, the pure, the powerful, and the positive. Having a positive attitude can make the difference between success and failure. Why? Well, I'm here to tell you! It's because a positive attitude and personal motivation allow you to remain excited about what you are doing—no matter how difficult the challenges may be from day to day. Show me somebody who isn't excited about what they are doing, and I'll show you somebody who is going to be "cooked in the squat!"

WHAT'S EXCITING ABOUT KNOWLEDGE?

Have you ever considered what gets you excited? I know you probably get excited when somebody gives you a great gift or a big raise. You also probably get excited when you think of something you can do that will help you become even more successful. You probably get excited when your team gets a big win or you close a deal you've been working on for awhile. Maybe you get excited when you see a new opportunity and are in a great position to take advantage of it. I remember how excited I got at the opportunity to marry the Redhead. That was more than sixty-five years ago, and it was possibly the greatest opportunity I ever had! I think you will agree that recognizing new opportunities is a source of excitement and also one of the best ways to remain optimistic and confident about your future. But let me ask you a question. How can you improve your ability to recognize good, new opportunities?

The amazing thing about opportunity is that it is in front of us every day, but it may elude us if we are not careful. For many people, opportunity is difficult to see. Knowledge, properly applied and acted upon, is the key to lifting the veil and opening your eyes to the opportunity that is in front of you. The more knowledge you have about a subject, the better equipped you become to link your daily experience to new opportunity. This is true because the human mind is designed to file away information and then subconsciously produce connections between seemingly

> THE MORE KNOWLEDGE YOU HAVE ABOUT A SUBJECT, THE BETTER EQUIPPED YOU BECOME TO LINK YOUR DAILY EXPERIENCE TO NEW OPPORTUNITY.

unrelated facts. If you haven't been learning new things and filing away new information on a regular basis, your mind will have difficulty making connections to new opportunities.

It's just a basic fact of life that it's hard to be positive and enthusiastic about something you know little about. That's why I have said in the past that it's generally true that *people are down on the things they're not "up on."* However, the worst-case scenario is to believe you are well versed in something when you are not. That circumstance will set you up for some seriously embarrassing moments!

Let's face it. If you don't know very much about something, chances are you are not going to be very interested in it. If you aren't interested in something, you won't be excited about it. For example, if you do not understand what a Smartphone can do for you or how it works, the likelihood of you investing the time and energy in learning to use one is pretty slim.

However, when you understand that a Smartphone can improve your communication with others, help you become better organized and more productive, and open the doors to powerful information in an instant, the value of the Smartphone is enhanced in your mind and becomes personally important. When you understand the benefits of using a Smartphone, your willingness to become a competent user increases. New knowledge becomes the motivating factor in learning how to use a Smartphone.

The kind of knowledge you need to become a good recognizer of new opportunity is not the issue. What matters is that you accept the importance of acquiring new knowledge and make it a life-long practice. As Paul Zane Pilzer, world-renowned economist, wisely states, "Prosperity belongs to those who learn new things the fastest." It is also well known that repetition is the mother of learning. I make it a point to do something every day to continually learn new things. I have always been a very prolific reader. As a matter of fact, for most of my life I have averaged reading about three hours a day. Every day I read the daily paper, and I also read my Bible. (That way I know what both sides are up to.) I also read great books, informative magazines, and numerous specialized publications. All of this reading continually adds to the knowledge I have.

As you probably know, I believe that you are what you are and where you are because of what goes into your mind. As I mentioned, I am also a strong supporter of "Automobile University." Listening to positive, informative programs and courses as you travel from one place to another can give you an otherwise unobtainable education. Thabiti Anyabwile, pastor of the First Baptist Church, Grand Cayman, said, "The use of time is important because time is the stuff of which days are made."

I have told you about the thousands of letters I have received from people all over the world thanking me for helping them. The truth of the matter is that I have never met the vast majority of these people. Most of them received my help by listening to my recorded tapes and CDs in their automobiles. This is particularly true of businesspeople and salespeople who travel a lot. They do not waste their time driving without adding to their knowledge base. Do you see your automobile as a rolling university? Technology today is such that you can import just about any information you need into your car via CDs, iPods, mp3 digital audio devices, iPads, etc. So take advantage of that time and put it to good use by listening to new information.

DON'T WASTE YOUR TIME

Earlier I said, "The kind of knowledge is not the issue." I want to revise that a bit, because sometimes we can fill our heads with knowledge that has very little value. Many years ago (when it was less risky than it is today), I had the opportunity to pick up a hitchhiker. When he got in the car, I began to believe I might have made a mistake, because he had obviously been drinking alcohol. He was also talking a lot. Eventually, the story came out that he had been recently released from prison. He had served eighteen months for bootlegging whiskey. Trying to be polite, I asked him if he had acquired any knowledge he could use when he was released. He assured me that he had. He said he had memorized the name of every county in every state in the United States. In addition, he had memorized all of the parishes in the state of Louisiana.

I had a difficult time believing what my hitchhiker had said to me so I decided to challenge him on his knowledge. Because I had lived in South Carolina and was familiar with many of the counties in that state, I asked him to name all the counties in South Carolina.

My hitchhiker proceeded to systematically recite all of the South Carolina counties. Now, I have no idea why this man selected this particular area of knowledge as something worth learning.

Maybe a bootlegger needs to know all the county jurisdictions of the sheriffs he is running from!

That's possibly useful for the bootlegger, but from a practical standpoint for folks like you and me, the information is probably useless. It might win you a bet, but it certainly isn't likely to help your career. I do not recommend investing the amount of time this man invested to memorize great amounts of minutiae. The knowledge you acquire should be relevant to your life and your interests. The key is to study a little bit every day, and this knowledge will help you recognize new opportunity.

I have touted the importance of being a lifetime learner for as long as I can remember, but the overwhelming majority of people appear to make a decision to stop learning anything by the time they reach the age of twenty-one and/or graduate from college! By that age, most people know how to perform the basic tasks of life. They know how to pay their bills (sometimes on time, sometimes not). They know how to drive a car. They know how to rent an apartment and carry on relationships with other people. And yet when it comes to learning anything new, it appears that they are resolutely opposed to reading a nonfiction book, learning about a new topic online, or otherwise enriching or increasing their knowledge base.

I know that you're not one of those people, but the reality is that far too many of us fail to take advantage of the myriad opportunities to keep learning and growing. In a country like ours where there are no limits on what information we can gain, what books we can read, or what websites we can visit, it's tragic that people don't make better use of their God-given minds.

I still wish I could sell you your brain for enough money that you would truly appreciate the incredible capacity your brain has for retaining and compartmentalizing the information you choose to store there. Many years ago, I said if I could charge you $100,000 to buy your brain from me, you would value it more. These days I'd probably have to charge you something like $100 million to make you appreciate the true value of your brain.

In fact, IBM spent hundreds of millions developing an artificial intelligence computer named Watson and then challenged the two biggest *Jeopardy*! game show winners to a contest in February 2011. Watson won.

If IBM believes investing huge amounts of time and money in artificial intelligence is smart and will pay off, can you imagine what you can do if you invest time to teach your real, truly intelligent brain new information?

WHO SUCCEEDS?

Individuals who understand the principle of having to make an investment in their lives before they can expect success are far more productive and proactively seek out the information and assistance they need to be successful in their endeavors. Individuals who keep growing in knowledge are the ones who succeed.

Doctors, for example, have to spend inordinate amounts of time reading and learning new things about their specialty. You might ask whether you would want to go to a doctor who stopped learning things twenty years ago. With the world changing as rapidly as it is, the people who are the most successful are the ones who have the greatest thirst for knowledge.

A TOOL FOR LIVING

Another fact about knowledge is that you have to understand it as a tool of life, and like any tool, you have to take care of it. Management expert Peter Drucker said, "Knowledge has to be improved, challenged, and increased constantly or it vanishes."

> INDIVIDUALS WHO KEEP GROWING IN KNOWLEDGE ARE THE ONES WHO SUCCEED.

A friend of mine once told me the details of the knowledge he gained in college many decades ago have largely vanished from his mind. He said his geology class was an example of vanishing information. When he took geology, he could recite all kinds of facts about the subject. He could identify types of rocks by sight and name them. Today, he retains nothing specific because he hasn't really thought about or used the information he learned in geology. The typing course he took is a different story! The advent of the computer age produced the opportunity to type every day, and for the past twenty years he has been improving and using his typing skills daily. He said typing may have been the most beneficial subject he took in college, from the standpoint of daily use and application.

You may be asking, "Zig, what does this have to do with me and my ability to win?" Well, the same holds true for any knowledge or skill you have or acquire in the future. If you use it, it will empower you. If you don't use it, you will lose it. So as you are preparing to win, it is very important that you understand that learning new things, acquiring knowledge, will make it possible for you to recognize opportunities as they are presented to you.

I have always found the Bible to be a great reservoir of applicable knowledge. I have also welcomed knowledge from my mentors like the late Fred Smith; my Jewish brother, Bernie Lofchick, and many others. Reading great books about great people allowed me to learn the principles they embraced that produced success in their lives. All of that knowledge became the tool I have used to recognize or reject new opportunity. If a new opportunity violates my principles, it is not an opportunity for me. As my friend and Ziglar, Inc., board member Billy Cox says, "You cannot go wrong doing what's right."

USING KNOWLEDGE TO DO WHAT'S RIGHT

Honesty is about the motives we have for doing things. It is about being faithful in our commitments to others. It involves what we are really thinking about things and what we believe about things. This is important because the knowledge we gain about honesty has the effect of becoming a filter for our choices about new opportunities. Knowledge has the power to help us avoid making bad choices that produce bad results. Let's say that you are looking for a job in sales and you respond to an ad that claims you can make $10,000 a month, working at home in your pajamas, investing very little effort. Because you have previously acquired knowledge that success requires making a real investment of time and effort, you will immediately recognize that the ad is deceptive at best and probably dishonest! Consequently, you won't waste time pursuing an opportunity that isn't right for you.

Suppose you have been working for an employer for a long time. In the course of your employment you have built many relationships with your employer's customers and also with your co-workers. Let's say someone approaches you one day and says they are starting a business just like your employer's. They offer you a big job with lots of money if you will go to work for them and bring a bunch of your employer's customers and his best employees with you. Does accepting that job offer violate the principles of loyalty that you have learned and accepted? I would say it most certainly does. But because you have knowledge about loyalty and understand how loyalty contributes to long-term success, you can filter out the new opportunity as not being right for you. You may think this example isn't very realistic, but I can assure you there are many people who have attempted to start a new business in exactly this way. There are also a great number of people who have accepted the opportunity—if you want to call it that.

Acquiring the knowledge of right and wrong in advance of the need to make a decision will ensure good choices and help you avoid pain, loss, grief, and regret.

TAKE THE TIME YOU NEED TO GET THE KNOWLEDGE YOU NEED

Everybody should set goals that will help them become equipped with the knowledge they need to be successful.

I believe a specific amount of time needs to be reserved every day for the acquisition of knowledge. When Theodore Roosevelt died, they found a book under his pillow. As I've said previously, I've been purposely reading non-fiction about three hours a day for many decades. The acquisition of knowledge has been a major goal of mine, and my hope is that it will become a significant goal for you.

CHAPTER SEVEN

PRACTICE PREPARES YOU FOR VICTORY

I love to use sports to teach and make significant points, and golf has been a sport in which I have actually participated much of my adult life. The unique thing about golf is that it is an individual sport, and literally anyone can become proficient enough to play a round of golf and enjoy it. Now, I'm not saying everyone will always be happy with the way they played or the score they achieved, but it is a game that can be enjoyable at many different skill levels. Millions of people play golf, and there are many thousands of players who are able to play and compete at the par and sub-par level. Par is the standard number of strokes expected from the best players to complete a round. Even though many people play the game and many people achieve excellence in their skill, only a tiny fraction of golfers manage to gain admittance to the professional game, and an even smaller fraction rises to the very top of the PGA tour.

When you watch a PGA tour event such as the Masters or the US Open Championship on television, there are always shots of various players at the practice tee or on a large green practicing their putting skills. These professionals usually invest multiple hours in practicing before the actual round of competitive golf begins. They will practice the same ten-foot putt over and over again, and then they will practice at another distance. The reason they practice so hard and so repetitively is because they know they will encounter similar putts during their actual round of play, and they want to be confident of making them when it matters. They are involved in practice without pressure so they can be ready to deliver when the pressure of competition is on.

The only thing I practiced more than my golf swing was the next speech I needed to give. I have been professionally delivering my message of hope, inspiration, and encouragement to large audiences for decades. I actually would be hard-pressed to even guess at the number of times I have made my presentation. But I did it long enough to know exactly what I was going to say, and I had the entire presentation burned into my mind. Throughout my career, I was able to give my presentation in various time frames. I could do fifteen minutes, thirty minutes, one hour, two hours, four hours, or *all day*! Whatever the length of any single event, I was able to give portions of my presentation word for word, the same way every time. If you heard me tell a specific story on one occasion and heard me tell the same story a few years later, chances are it would be almost identical to the first time you heard it. Why? Well, I've spent a lot of time thinking about every word I say and the order of what I say. I've thought about the voice inflections I use on certain words, and I know I am saying what I need to say in the most effective way possible. My presentation is polished to a very high level, and it happened because of hundreds of hours of intense practice!

You may be surprised to know that even though I had my presentation deeply engrained in my mind, I still practiced for several hours before every speech I delivered. In addition to the stories and examples I liked to relate, I used current information and material to keep the messages interesting and relevant. When I traveled, I had all my notes and points in front of me and went over them, saying the words in my mind and with my voice. I knew the worst thing I could do would be to think I knew my presentation so well that I didn't have to practice. That would be the point at which the quality and effectiveness of the presentation would have begun to change for the worse—and I knew it. In the same way, if a professional golfer stops practicing, his quality of play will begin to erode and his competitive edge will diminish. Practice prepares professional golfers and professional speakers for victory, and practice will prepare you for victory, too!

DOING NEW THINGS

The *Born to Win* process will inevitably lead you into doing new things. Doing new things involves change, and change is something lots of people avoid because of the fear of failure. In fact, the fear of failure is often strong enough to keep some people from taking the first step. They get "cooked in the squat" and procrastinate themselves into a perpetual process of just "getting ready" to do what they committed to do. The fear of failure is a serious condition, and there may be many reasons for it. Some of them may be complicated, but there is one reason that covers about 95 percent of those fears, and that reason can be overcome simply, quickly, and effectively. What is that reason? It's simply fear of the unknown. This is the fear that results from being unfamiliar with the thing you are going to be doing.

Think of all the things you do every day that you do automatically and don't even have to think about doing. Even though they are easily done today, they began as fearful experiences. For example, we all remember the fear and trepidation we experienced learning to ride a bicycle. You may have avoided getting on the bike because you were afraid of falling off and injuring yourself. Then you finally got up the courage to attempt your first ride—and you fell off! Repeated practice allowed you to eventually master your bike-riding skills, and you then became so confident in your ability you could jump on the bike with no fear or concern. That principle works in anything we do. We have to practice, and that makes us competent. When we become competent, we do not fear failure!

Marc Yu is an eleven-year-old piano prodigy who lives in California. Marc has been playing the piano as long as he can remember. When he was three years old, he could play a Sonatina in G Major by Beethoven. When Marc Yu was nine, he played a Chopin composition written for the benefit of earthquake victims in Sichuan, China. This young phenomenon practices as many as eight hours a day. Marc himself says, "Practice makes perfect." Marc's success is the result of lots of natural ability coupled with the discipline of daily practice. The 2010 World Expo was held in Shanghai, China. The United States had a booth there featuring an exhibition on "The Chinese in America." Marc was one of twenty Chinese-Americans to be showcased in that venue. He shared the spotlight with such great people as I.M. Pei, Yo-Yo Ma, and others. Not bad for an eleven-year-old boy who learned the value of practice at a very early age.

There are many very successful and famous people who were born with certain gifts and abilities like Marc Yu. Most people, however, are not born with skills that destine them to be prodigies. Most people are born with an average amount of intelligence and an average amount of ability. I'm included in that group. My wife was ranked fourth in a high school class of three hundred. I was in the part of the class that made the top half possible! Whatever success I have enjoyed as a speaker and author was not the result of some natural talent. My success was the result of hard work and practice, and what I practiced was very specific. I practiced my speaking and communication skills for the purpose of being the best speaker I could be. Malcolm Gladwell in his book *Outliers* lays out a compelling case that in almost every instance, it takes ten thousand hours of practice and hard work to be a superstar and an elite performer at the very top of their game. Three British researchers, Michael J. Howe, Jane W. Davidson, and John A. Sluboda, wrote a huge report in 2006 that dealt with the causes of excellence. Their study proved that people who excelled did not achieve their excellence because they were gifted with innate gifts. In fact, their research exposed that most people can learn the basics of things fairly quickly, but most of them peak out at a level of proficiency they are satisfied with. That is what happened to me in my golf game. I got good enough to make me happy, and that is when my golf lessons got further and further apart. But the study reported that a very small percentage of people never peak, and they just keep on learning and improving for years—those are the people who go on to unique success and eventually stardom.

YOU HAVE TO PRACTICE THE LITTLE THINGS

> BECAUSE SUCCESS OR FAILURE FREQUENTLY DEPENDS ON THE LITTLE THINGS, IT IS IMPERATIVE THAT YOU PRACTICE THEM.

Are you convinced that what makes people great is practice? The question is this: What is the best kind of practice? I want to help you with the hard ones, so the correct answer is the "little things." The little things in life frequently make the difference in success and failure. If you are in sales, for example, you are very familiar with the lost opportunities that may have turned on a single word or phrase. Or maybe the sale was lost because a point was omitted or not stated clearly.

Because success or failure frequently depends on the little things, it is imperative that you practice them.

Since I mentioned sales, let me give you an example of a little thing I regularly practiced. Every salesperson or entrepreneur understands that sales are not completed until both parties sign a contract or an order. So the signing of something is very important, and as a salesperson you want to plant suggestions that signing is important. In order to introduce the concept of signing to my prospects, I frequently told stories that involved signing things. I would practice telling those stories over and over again, placing emphasis on the word *sign*. Following are the words that I would practice:

"Many years ago, God gave me a beautiful woman, and I'm one of the truly fortunate men in that I love her infinitely more today than I did the day I got her. I got her because one day, in the presence of witnesses, the minister, and Almighty God, I signed my name. I had four beautiful children—three daughters and a son. They were all mine, but the doctor would not even let me take them out of the hospital until I had signed my name. I own a lot of life insurance. I bought it because I wanted to make certain if anything happened to me my family's standard of living would not decline and my wife would not have to go to work unless she wanted to. I was able to protect my family's financial future because on several different occasions, in the presence of a competent salesperson, I signed my name. As a matter of fact, Mr. Prospect, I've never made any progress of any kind, anywhere, or an acquisition of anything of value, until I committed myself by signing my name. Mr. Prospect, if I'm reading you right—and I think I am—you're the kind of person who not only likes to make progress but who also likes to do things for your family. You can do both of those things right now by signing your name."

If you have ever sold anybody anything, you know that closing the sale and getting their signature on the bottom line is frequently the most awkward and difficult part of the sales presentation. Many salespeople start thinking about the close before they have finished demonstrating their product. This can create nervousness for them. They might be unsure about what they will say; they might be uncertain about how they will transfer their customer's obvious desire for the product into a signed agreement. Because I memorized and practiced the example I just gave about signing my name, I always knew exactly what I was going to say, so I was never nervous about moving to the close. Because I practiced placing emphasis on the word *sign,* I was confident my customer would be ready to buy and sign my agreement. It was the practice that gave me the confidence to overcome a potentially difficult moment, because I had done it so many times before. So practice the little things, because they are the things that make a big difference.

WHAT KINDS OF THINGS CAN YOU PRACTICE?

Now you might be thinking, "Zig, I'm not a salesman, so what should I practice?" You might even be thinking, "Isn't there a limit to the kinds of things you can practice?" Practice is simply preparation for success. I want to tell you very clearly and plainly that you can practice anything to create and reinforce good, positive habits. *Born to Win* is about planning, preparing, and expecting to win. It is also about being the best you can be, no matter your job or profession. If you are a flagman on

> PRACTICE IS SIMPLY PREPARATION FOR SUCCESS.

a road construction crew, you can practice to become the best flagman that road crew ever had. Instead of slouching against a pickup truck and frowning at the people passing through, you can practice having a smile on your face. You can stand in front of a mirror with your flag and get a visual picture of the posture you want to have on the job. You can practice waving your flag in a professional, crisp, but friendly motion. You can practice tipping your hat and smiling at your customers as they drive past you. When you practice those gestures and take them to the road, you're going to make a powerful impression on the people driving by and the people you work with. One of the people you impress will be the boss who assigned you to flag duty in the first place. Your outstanding performance, based on your practice, might even get you a promotion.

I hope you get the point that you can practice anything! Perhaps you are a stay-at-home mom, home-schooling your children. Possibly there is a certain piece of curriculum that makes you uncomfortable when you present it. To overcome that, just practice that portion of the curriculum over and over again until you have it down exactly as you want to say it. Literally, if you prepare in advance to succeed by practicing, everything can be improved.

To determine what you need to practice, take a look at your goals and identify the specific things that will require you to improve your skills. Pay particular attention to the items that make you feel a bit uncomfortable because it is something you aren't used to doing. Those are the things you need to begin to practice regularly. Make a list of all those things and then think about creating exercises you can practice that will produce the improvement you want. Then set aside a little time each day to practice those exercises until you have mastered them.

Practice doesn't just make perfect. Practice also creates competence, confidence, clarity, certainty, and success.

CHAPTER EIGHT

GET THE RIGHT ADVICE

As I said previously, there is no substitute for experience, and there are two ways you can acquire experience. One is to go out and do things, and the other is to benefit from the experience of others! It can be a lot less costly to learn from others' mistakes—and successes! We all need guidance from time to time, and it's critically important that you keep your mind open to listening to the wisdom of others and have the courage to apply it to your own life for success. For some reason, however, many people have problems taking advice. They are stubbornly committed to their own way, regardless of the results they may be getting.

Milton Dicus, a mentor to my trusted and wise editor on this book, Michael Levin, says that demigods have yes men, but statesmen have advisors. In other words, despots never take advice from anyone, and anyone foolhardy enough to give truthful advice to such a leader is likely to find himself put to death for his troubles. By contrast, a statesman or leader is someone who seeks out wise counsel from others.

Gavin de Becker is one of the leading security advisors in the world. He wrote a book called *The Gift of Fear*. In it, he says that we humans only second-guess ourselves when we're right. When we're wrong, we get very stubborn, and we won't take advice from anybody! The lesson here is that when we feel absolutely certain of our position and we feel we don't need guidance from anybody at all, that's the time we most need advice!

Doris Kearns Goodwin, in her book *Team of Rivals*, points out Abraham Lincoln's extreme humility in that he put the very people who had opposed him the most vociferously in the presidential campaign as his main advisors, because he knew they had plenty of wisdom to share despite the things that they had said about him during the campaign. It takes courage and humility to seek advice, especially from people who might have been our opponents at one time!

BE AN ADVICE MINER

It's vitally important that we become skilled "advice miners" and that we realize that getting advice from others has a good side and a bad side. It's kind of like mining for gold. Most of the material removed from a gold mine isn't worth much until it has been crushed, sifted, washed, and filtered. When that has been done, what is left is the gold. Good advice is like gold and is just as valuable. But there is a lot of advice that needs to be discarded like the leftover rocks and mud in the gold mining process. The problem with bad advice is that it can have a toxic effect on your life and take you down paths you should not be traveling.

I sought out men with high moral values who put as much importance on learning as I did to be my mentors. Many of my mentors were known to be top advisors in their field of knowledge. If you want good input, you need to go to the best. I asked the late Fred Smith to be my mentor after I had several business meetings with him and saw how he handled all issues with integrity and an unparalleled sense of fairness.

If you ask someone to be your mentor and they aren't able to mentor you, they will let you know. They will be honored that you asked and, in most cases, will agree to give you enough advice to get you headed in the right direction.

As a young boy, Victor Serebriakoff got some bad advice from one of his teachers that had a profound impact on his life. When Victor was fifteen, the teacher told him he would probably never finish school. The advice given to Victor was to drop out of school and just go learn a manual trade or skill. Victor believed the teacher, and for the next seventeen years he drifted around doing odd jobs, believing he was the "dunce" the teacher had told him he was.

When Victor was in his early thirties, he happened to take an IQ test that revealed he was far from being a "dunce." In fact, he had an IQ of 161! He immediately started acting like the genius he was and became an author, secured several patents, and was very successful in business. He also became one of the leaders of an organization called Mensa (for people who have an IQ over 140). The point of this story is that some bad advice caused Victor to fall short of his potential for seventeen years!

Good advice can have exactly the opposite effect. I've often told the story of how P.C. Merrell changed my life with some good advice. He told me I could be a champion if I just applied myself consistently and believed that I could accomplish my goals. That advice put me on a path that led to everything I have said or done since. There are many others who gave me life-changing advice. As a matter of fact, I have photographs of each one of them hanging on the wall of my office that I call my *Wall of Gratitude*. Each person on that wall gave me great advice that I accepted and used to grow my spiritual, physical, family and business life. Just so you don't think all the advice I've taken was perfect, I need to confess that I've been given bad advice, too (which I took), and the results weren't that great—as a matter of fact, the results were terrible! I say this so you will know I've had good advice and bad advice, and through the years I've learned to know the difference. I know how to spot good givers of advice (often called mentors or, these days, coaches) and I'm going to tell you how to do the same. I've come to see there are seven solid characteristics of good coaches, and when you take advice from someone, be sure they have as many of these characteristics as possible.

THE SEVEN CHARACTERISTICS OF GOOD PERSONAL COACHES

1. They have good character

Good advice is like a good piece of fruit. Personally, I *love* peaches. Just thinking about the juicy goodness of a freshly picked, ripe peach makes my mouth start watering. But if, in the process of eating that peach, I find a couple of worms and a rotten spot, it changes the entire experience. Advice is the same. If the person doing the coaching has good character, taking the advice they offer can be a wonderful experience. If they have character that is not so good, their advice can lead to a bad experience.

Character is about the sum total of a person, and it is the result of the habits a person builds on a daily basis. It reflects their honesty, their dependability, and whether they are trustworthy. A person with good character keeps their word, and they want the best for others. They are not self-centered or self-seeking. You can see why advice from a person with bad character can and should be suspect. I've always said that ability can take you to the top, but it takes character to keep you there!

Good character makes a person dependable and trustworthy. Those are the kinds of people you want as advisors. The late J. P. Morgan was asked what he considered to be the best bank collateral. Without hesitation he replied, "Character."

William Lake put it this way: "One of the most important lessons that experience teaches is that, on the whole, success depends more upon character than either intellect or fortune." So, when looking for a good coach, first examine their character.

2. They have a track record of success

Taking advice from someone who has no track record of success is a bad strategy. You can learn from the mistakes others have made, but if you want coaching about positive things you can do to be successful, look for that advice from people who have been and are successful. If you want to know how to win at something, talk to people who have been winners doing the same thing. I know this seems obvious, but sometimes it can be tricky to determine if a person really has a track record of success. I am generally pretty suspicious of people who blow their own horn trying to convince me how successful they have been. I'm talking about the kind of person you meet who immediately starts dropping names and going on and on about all the great things they have done. Self-proclaimed success is not a reliable measuring stick to determine if a person really has a good track record.

People who are successful do not have to sell themselves that hard. You hear of their success from others, and you see it as you learn more and more about their lives and their circumstances. What this means is that you need to get to know someone pretty well before you start taking their advice.

Through the years we've learned the importance of fully checking out resumes and even digging deeply enough to learn if someone has actually graduated from the university they list on their job application. I have been surprised at the number of jobs people leave off of their applications and how easy it is for someone's effervescent personality to make you doubt the truth of anything negative you might discover. It's easy to be drawn into liking someone immediately and then find yourself trying to justify hiring someone who has not been completely honest in their interview.

Let the evidence speak for itself. If you are taking advice from or considering working with someone and you learn they have not been honest about themselves, please understand this is a character flaw that you are not likely to change any time soon. The moral is to look beyond the surface and what people say about themselves.

Facebook has brought this stark reality home to far too many people already! Personal behavior and photography that seemed fun and silly when posted by a twenty-year-old can become the stuff of missed job opportunities further down the road. Smart employers are increasingly looking at Facebook and other social media tools to help them make decisions about hiring..

3. They are good listeners

You have heard the saying that "God gave us two ears and one mouth for a reason!" Did you know you don't learn a thing when your mouth is moving? That may sound funny coming from a guy who consistently speaks at the rate of two hundred fifty words a minute with gusts up to four hundred, but it's true.

What you may not know is that I'm a pretty good listener, and the things I've learned listening through the years have given me the ammunition I need to talk so much. I really love to listen to smart people, and I spend much of my time doing just that. I always carry a notepad and a pen so I can write down the good information I hear.

It is important that your advisors/coaches be good listeners. A wise man once said, "Talking is sharing but listening is caring." You want your advisors to really care about you and your success, so it's important that they be good listeners not only to get to know you but also to understand what you really need and how they can help you. A good coach is really an encourager, and to be a good encourager, you have to be a good listener.

Identifying a good listener is pretty easy. They maintain good eye contact, and their facial expressions demonstrate interest in what you are saying. They are not rolling their eyes and looking all around the room. They are not texting on their phone or answering email. If their phone rings while they are in a serious conversation with you, they ignore the call. Good listeners are also interested in learning from others, and they know that the first step in that process is to shut their mouth and open their ears.

4. They are good decision makers

I'm amazed at how little thought is given to making decisions. How decisions are made, why decisions are made, and when decisions are made is often taken for granted. Everyone expects to think seriously about decisions like marriage, having a child, or accepting a job offer that moves them hundreds of miles away from family, but they give little thought to the actual process of decision-making and the basis for making good decisions. It takes time to learn to consistently make good decisions, because good decisions require a certain amount of wisdom. That's why a good decision maker can offer you advice that you can trust.

Great advisors and coaches consistently make good decisions and good choices because they have acquired a good deal of wisdom throughout their lives. How do you acquire wisdom, and how does it work in the decision-making process? Wisdom is acquired by gaining knowledge and learning to apply that knowledge to the daily events of life. The daily events of life are filled with decisions, and these choices create the results of our lives. The kind of knowledge that creates wisdom is information that is true and correct. Information that is false is not authentic knowledge, and because it is false, it is not wisdom. Lots of people acquire false information, believe it is true, and make bad decisions as a result of that information.

People who make good decisions have the ability to test the information they get and filter out the parts that are not true. This ability leads to the skill of good decision making. These are the kinds of people you want as advisors and coaches. People who are good decision makers can help you develop the ability to test bad information and reject it. When you develop this ability, you, too, will become a good decision maker.

5. They tell the truth (even when it hurts)

A good coach cares more about giving you the right information you need than worrying that what they say might offend you or hurt your feelings. After all, you don't look for advice for the purpose of getting compliments and accolades (although some people do exactly that). A good advisor must be truthful with themselves and others, and the inability to do that makes for someone you absolutely don't want advice from.

One of the greatest advisors I had in my life was my mother, and she had some strong opinions about telling the truth. She also taught me the importance of absolute integrity, faith, hard work, responsibility, love, and commitment. She was actually my first and greatest role model. She had many life-shaping sayings that remain so fresh in my mind that I can recall them in the sound of her very voice. Concerning telling the truth I can still hear her saying, "Tell the truth and tell it ever, costeth what it will; for he who hides the wrong he did, does the wrong thing still." Then Mama would slap her hand down on the table and say, "If a man finds out that your word is no good, he'll soon know that neither are you!" Now, that's the kind of advisor you need to help you succeed in life and in business.

6. They have good personal relationships

Nothing says more about a person than the quality of the relationships they enjoy. When you see someone who has great relationships with their family members and they have friendships that have survived through many years, it means they have been doing lots of things correctly. Good advisors don't mind investing their time and knowledge in you because they have a history of long-term relationships built on a foundation of caring for and helping others. Unfortunately, the availability of good advisors may be more limited now than it has been in years past. The inability to have good relationships has escalated dramatically in the last thirty years. Modern American society has become rude and self-centered; its philosophy has become, "Hooray for me, to heck with you, I'm going to do it my way. I'll win through intimidation. I'm going to look out for Number One, and I'm going to do it now." That philosophy quite accurately depicts a miserable human being. I, personally, have never met a happy self-centered person, and I'll bet that you haven't, either.

Misery is the only emotion left for people who have alienated everyone around them. Manipulating and intimidating people, disregarding their needs, and always putting yourself first will make you a lonely person. People who have trouble fostering relationships spend a lot of time alone, and quite simply, lonely people are miserable people. You don't want an advisor who is miserable and self-centered. Look for people who have lots of good relationships, because they probably care a lot about others, and they will care about you, too.

7. They celebrate the success of others

Why would you want to take the advice of someone who would enjoy watching you fail? They are the kind of people who would put a tax on the milk of human kindness! Believe it or not, there are lots of people who find satisfaction in the failure of others, and they actively try to help others fail. I have written before about my youngest daughter, Julie, who became separated from her husband, Jim. Of all the women she knew, only one encouraged her to do the hard work of trying to fix their marriage. All the rest advised her to go ahead with her life and move on without him. Fortunately, Julie took the advice of the friend who encouraged her, and in 2011, she and Jim celebrated their twenty-eighth wedding anniversary. Their success at healing their marriage has been an inspiration for many others, and whenever Julie or Jim encounters someone considering divorce, they encourage and advise couples to stick it out and work through their issues. They want others to be as successful as they were in overcoming adversity and problems.

You do not want to become a SNIOP (once again, a person **S**usceptible to the **N**egative **I**nfluence of **O**ther **P**eople). Let's face it, people who are unable to encourage you in your vision or dream and instead tell you all the things they don't believe you can do or accomplish are negative influences. Run from those folks as fast as you can, because they do not wish the best for you. Instead, look for advice from people who celebrate the success of others. They are natural cheerleaders and get a real kick out of seeing anyone do well.

It would be an ideal situation if all of your advisors and coaches could be credited with all seven of these characteristics I've shared with you. This is why Jim Rohn said, "Everyone should have at least six mentors." Pick out their best qualities and implement them into your own life; build others and use them to help you become the winner you were born to be. What you don't want to do is to take advice from anyone who doesn't seem to have any of the seven characteristics we discussed! Don't look for people who will tell you what you want to hear. Look for people who will truthfully share their wisdom with you, because they want you to succeed as they have succeeded.

To become willing to seek the advice you need to help you may be one of the greatest skills you can acquire in your life. No person has all the information or skill they need to maximize their potential. We all need help and assistance from others in some way. As a matter of fact, you would be hard-pressed to think of anything you have that did not involve help from another person. If you have a job, someone hired you. If you drive a car, someone probably made you a car loan to finance it. If you own a house, someone gave you a mortgage. If you have a great wife, she had to agree to being your life partner. I think you get the point. We all need the cooperation and assistance of others, and good advice is part of that assistance. If you want to be all you can be, take good advice from good people. When you do that consistently, you will be equipped to win!

Part Three
Expecting to Win

CHAPTER NINE

EXPECT TO WIN

Have you ever wondered about the difference between people who win consistently and people who lose consistently? Some of it relates to the talent they have (or don't have). Some of it relates to how well they planned and prepared to win. But much of the difference relates to how convinced they become about their ability to win! To be really clear about this, winners expect to win, they expect victory, and they expect success! Expecting to win is not just a matter of thinking you will win and willing it to happen (although that is important). Expecting to win is a right that must be earned, and there are some things you must do to earn that right.

There is a significant difference between people who do great things and people who don't. People who accomplish great things work toward their objectives every day. You see, planning, preparing, and expecting—all three work together to create winning results. Expecting is not the ending... it's simply the third ingredient in winning. And it's something you must do and improve on constantly. Stop planning, stop preparing, and you stop winning. Very simply put, a competitive weight lifter who chose to lie on the beach for six months could not show up at a competition and legitimately expect to win.

No, they must plan to win by setting their goals and getting a plan of action. They must prepare to win by following that plan and working daily to strengthen and build their muscles. Then they can legitimately expect to have a shot at winning. A parent cannot ignore the behavior of their children, fail to discipline them or fail to reward them, and expect to produce a disciplined, loving, responsible adult. A daily investment must be made in the child's life to prepare them by teaching them and guiding them into becoming all they can be. To earn the right to expect success (in anything you do), you must have a daily objective to make an honest effort to continue to plan better and be better prepared for today than you were yesterday. If you pay that price daily by planning and preparing and working to become the right kind of person, then you can legitimately expect to have all that life has to offer.

THE THREE DIMENSIONS OF LIFE

There are three dimensions in every person's life that must be nurtured and disciplined daily if you hope to earn the right to expect success. The first dimension is spiritual, the second dimension is mental, and the third dimension is physical. Each dimension is separate from the others, but they all work together to make up the total person. If any of these dimensions is neglected in the planning and preparing, the right to expect success will be limited.

The Spiritual Dimension

The spiritual dimension of your life is the most important, but it is frequently the most neglected. It is so important I can state with confidence that your spiritual condition is the controlling factor behind all that you will be or become. For it is out of our souls that our attitude flows, and your attitude will determine your altitude in life. The depth of your spirit will determine the height of your success. How do I know this is true? Before I began to concentrate on my own spiritual condition, I was broke and in debt. I had periods of limited success but could not sustain them and build anything meaningful. After I discovered my spiritual needs and began to take my faith seriously, everything changed. My speaking career took off and everything in my life took on a deeper, more meaningful purpose.

FOR IT IS OUT OF OUR SOULS THAT OUR ATTITUDE FLOWS, AND YOUR ATTITUDE WILL DETERMINE YOUR ALTITUDE IN LIFE. THE DEPTH OF YOUR SPIRIT WILL DETERMINE THE HEIGHT OF YOUR SUCCESS.

Why is your spirituality so important? It's really simple. You are a spiritual creature at the core of your being, and there are specific guidelines for operating your equipment (your life). Many people believe that humans are just a more intelligent form of animal life, but that isn't very logical, based on the observable facts and the track record of human beings. The difference between human beings and animal life is profound. Animals are driven and motivated by two things: survival and reproduction. Human beings break the mold of this model because our behavior is driven as much by what we *believe* as what we need. The things we believe drive our thinking; our thoughts produce emotions that influence our choices; and our choices determine what we do and how we live. In this respect, people are primarily driven and motivated by faith (what they believe).

Human beings have a deep, basic need for hope and love. Human beings will give their lives for intangible ideas and principles. Human beings spend their lives seeking things that will make them "happy" and provide a state of internal peace and serenity. Animals don't behave that way.

These intangible qualities and needs move the human being out of the animal kingdom and add another dimension to existence. These are spiritual qualities, not biological traits. During the earthly ministry of Jesus Christ, He confirmed this idea and said we are capable of attaining and receiving eternal life. A biological organism will not live forever. All biological creatures die, because the physical body eventually wears out or is destroyed. Only the spiritual part of a person has the potential to transcend death of the physical body. If you believe you are a spiritual creature and are more than an animal, it's pretty important that you begin to nurture your spiritual dimension and operate your spiritual equipment the way it is supposed to be operated. That's just basic common sense. When you buy a new car, you get an owner 's manual with it that explains in detail how to take care of the car, keep it in top condition, and what to do when it breaks down. If you follow the maintenance schedule in the manual, your car will operate smoothly and efficiently for many years.

In much the same way, we need to understand how to take care of and nurture our spiritual equipment. Since our spirituality is the most central component of our existence, it's easy to see that a well-maintained spiritual life will produce a better life overall. Otherwise, you will wind up living and thinking like an animal!

The Mental Dimension

The human mind is an amazing machine, but it must be cared for and given a lot of attention. As a matter of fact, you are what you think, and you become what you think. If you want to change your life, you have to change what goes into your mind! In other words, if you want to be a winner, you have to think like a winner.

Our mental abilities are housed in our brains, and if you think of your brain as a muscle, you can see the importance of exercising it daily to keep it in top condition. The best exercise for the brain (and your mind) is to force it to think! Thinking may sound like something that is easy, but the kind of thinking I'm talking about requires effort. Let's go back to the muscle concept, and I believe you will completely understand what I'm talking about.

When you go to the gym to exercise your body, a good trainer will tell you that your exercise program should be designed to build up your cardiovascular (heart and lungs) system and to build muscle. Cardio-vascular improvement comes by way of elevating the heart rate for longer and longer periods of time. Each day, the goal is to go a little longer on the treadmill or the stair-climbing machine. You may start out with a ten-minute routine before you are exhausted, but before long you can easily go thirty minutes or even an hour at faster and faster paces. If you have ever done cardio work, you also know that it is uncomfortable when you begin to reach your point of exhaustion, but when you push through the pain, you always achieve a higher level of endurance.

Muscle building also requires some pain and exhaustion, because muscle tissue builds through repetitive lifting of increasingly heavy weights. The interesting thing about muscle building is that it doesn't hurt while you are doing it. The soreness is an after-effect, as the muscles actually tear a little in response to the exercise and begin to rebuild even stronger new muscle. In this case, the time-worn saying "no pain, no gain" certainly holds true. Exercising your brain muscle is much the same from the standpoint of the daily need to exercise. The pain of exercising your brain comes in the form of being forced to think in ways that might be a bit uncomfortable.

To exercise your brain and challenge it to think, there are two things you need to do daily to be successful. The first is to continually add new information that your brain can process. New information comes by way of listening and observing. It also comes by way of reading. So the first step of brain exercise is to spend a little time each day soaking up new information through reading some good material or listening to audio messages by people who have knowledge you don't have. This is why "Automobile University" (listening to audio material while commuting) is such an effective way to get new information.

The second objective in brain exercise is processing all the new information you gain and applying it to your life. This happens as you think about all you have learned and force yourself to use that information to set goals that cause you to stretch out of your comfort zone and take new actions that will make a difference in the way you live. Because information today is literally at our fingertips, lots of people believe they suffer from information overload. They have a lot more information than they can possibly use, and they invest too little time and effort in the thought process of how to apply what they have gleaned in their lives. For this reason we need step two in our brain exercise program: spending quiet time with yourself solely for the purpose of thinking and meditating. It is during this quiet time that you should focus on new, creative ideas and solutions to the problems you may encounter. Take this time to clearly visualize the desired outcome and results you want in all areas of your business and personal life.

My friend and mentor, the late Fred Smith, planted this thought in my mind (the need for daily quiet time), and as a result I made a significant change in my daily routine. Interestingly, it involved my daily exercise regimen. For many years I ran, jogged, and walked daily based on the advice of my doctor friend, Dr. Kenneth Cooper. Before Fred Smith planted the idea of having some daily time to just think and meditate, I listened to cassette recordings while running or walking. After Fred's suggestion, it occurred to me that I could turn my walking and running into a time of focused thinking. I can tell you that once I started doing this I began to develop some of my most creative ideas. However, no matter how you find and allocate the time, just be sure to set aside time daily to be quiet and think. It can be early in the morning, during the day, or late at night. You can be walking, sitting, or lying down, but you need a specific thinking agenda. Think about projects or problems you are working on and explore how the new information you have acquired can be applied to those situations. You will be amazed at the immediate increase in not only your creativity, but in your productivity as well.

The Physical Dimension

It probably seems like I covered much of the physical dimension during the segment that discussed exercising the brain, and I did. But there is more to the physical dimension than just exercise. While it is the mind and spirit that make human beings unique in creation, they require a biological container in which to live. You can have the greatest mind in the world and you can be spiritually fit, but neglect of the physical body can cut short or limit your effectiveness and your success.

I'm not saying that people who have physical limitations won't be successful. Countless thousands of physically impaired people do extraordinary things every day and serve as an inspiration to others. Achilles International, for example, makes it possible for disabled runners, including blind, deaf, quadriplegic, and paraplegic athletes, to complete the New York City Marathon and other distance events around the world. The individuals who compete with the help of Achilles International complete a physical act of endurance and courage that most able-bodied people never accomplish.

What I am saying is that care of your physical equipment is a choice, and if you choose to care for your body and keep it healthy, you will be in a much better position to maximize your potential and therefore your success. The person who makes a million dollars and ruins his health along the way is not a success.

How important is your health to you? If you've always had good health, it is far more important than you might know! You've probably heard it said that our health is our greatest wealth. Many people give up their health to gain wealth. Having done so, they quickly realize that they would gladly exchange all their wealth to regain even some of their health. When we are young and vigorous, we frequently take our good health for granted and believe we will never face serious illness, injury, or some other debilitating condition. When many people think of success, they think of money and the things that money can buy. Well, money can buy you a bed, but it won't buy you a good night's sleep. Money can buy you a house but not a home.

Money can buy pleasure but not happiness. Money won't buy you good health either, but is good health a priority in your life? Would you trade places with a person who was severely injured in an accident, lost their legs, and received a $1 million insurance settlement? If you answered "no," then you obviously value your health more than money!

When I was a younger man, I weighed well over two hundred pounds and was really out of shape. When the day came that I fully embraced the need to lose weight and start taking care of myself, it was hard to change the way I had been living but well worth the effort. In 2010, I celebrated eighty-four years of life and I was still traveling and speaking to large audiences. My short-term memory failed me, and my body failed me too at times, but I still enjoyed my life and the things I was doing. Even though I no longer travel and speak publicly, I am still able to do much of what I do as the direct result of the diet and exercise program I have followed for the past forty years. The aging process is unstoppable, and someday we will all pass from this world and meet our Maker, but the quality of life for an aging person is directly related to how well they cared for their bodies in their younger years. I am so grateful I am now reaping the benefits of my decision all those decades ago to change my lifestyle.

Do you have a good eating and weight control plan? Do you do some physical exercise every day? If you want to provide your spirit and your mind a top-notch house to live in, you will do both! I urge you to set some goals today to give your body the attention and care it deserves.

THE RIGHT TO EXPECT TO WIN

I promise that you will have earned the right to expect to win if you understand the tri-dimensional nature of your life. Daily attention to the spiritual, mental, and physical areas of your life will pay huge dividends over the long haul. You will be more confident. You will be at peace with yourself and with others. You will have boundless energy to tackle the challenges of life and overcome them. With all that going for you, it is no wonder that you will have earned the right to expect to win!

CHAPTER TEN

THE POWER OF ENCOURAGEMENT AND HOPE

Let me ask you a question. Do you believe that I have been relatively successful in my speaking career? I don't want to be guilty of tooting my own horn, but it is a fact that I have had the privilege of making live presentations to literally millions of people around the world over the past forty years. I have also authored thirty books, many of which have been translated into different dialects and languages. Those accomplishments and facts about my career far exceed any dreams I may have had as young boy growing up in Yazoo City, Mississippi, during the Great Depression.

Let me ask you another question. If you could make one statement that describes what I have been able to do in my career that led to my success, what would you say? Would you say it was because of my ability to speak at the rate of two hundred fifty words per minute with gusts of up to four hundred? Would you say it's because I taught great sales programs to salespeople? Would you say it's because of what some call my sparkling personality? I hope at least a few of those things are true, but the real accomplishment of my career was to be an encourager to others. As I am in the ninth decade of my life, I clearly see today that encouragement and hope are the two most powerful qualities any person can provide to others. This is true because encouragement and hope are critical to success: they are the fuel of confidence and the engine of positive thinking and attitude.

THIS IS TRUE BECAUSE ENCOURAGEMENT AND HOPE ARE CRITICAL TO SUCCESS: THEY ARE THE FUEL OF CONFIDENCE AND THE ENGINE OF POSITIVE THINKING AND ATTITUDE.

During my career I have had the pleasure of meeting thousands of people who have been encouraged by my books and audio recordings. For years I have received personal letters from many of them sharing how encouragement changed their life. Each of them has a similar story, and their story of success begins with being encouraged and given hope that they might be able to accomplish more than they thought possible in their lives. I've seen and met people who have been pulled from total disaster because of encouragement. By being encouraged, they came to see and believe that they had hope for a better life, a better physical condition, better personal relation-ships, and a better spiritual relationship with God. In some cases, encouragement can be elusive, and it is hard to identify the specific thing that gave encouragement to someone who did not have it. But it is usually nothing more than a person being able to completely change a fundamental belief about himself and then allowing that belief to blossom into full-blown hope!

WHAT IS HOPE?

Hope is the power that gives a person the confidence to step out and try.

Understanding hope is really pretty simple. When you have hope, you believe that something good is going to happen in the future, even though it seems unlikely. Hope is a unique human emotion that has the power to transcend grief, disaster, and calamity. Hope has the power to change your mind and your thinking and produce new optimism where none had existed. Hope is the intangible quality of human existence that has the power to revive and give you the strength to do what you must do, in spite of circumstances. Without hope, there is depression, stagnation, and negative thought processes that can paralyze you emotionally.

In my book *Confessions of a Grieving Christian*, I shared the most catastrophic event of my life. I wrote that book out of grief for my oldest daughter, Suzan. She died of pulmonary fibrosis at the age of forty-six, and it was the toughest experience of my entire life. But her death was also one of the greatest stories of hope I have ever experienced.

During the last two weeks of Suzan's life she was in the intensive care unit (ICU) at St. Paul's Hospital in Dallas. Virtually all of the patients in that unit were in life-threateningly critical condition. Our family stayed together and was present in the ICU for the entire ordeal of Suzan's last days, and we had the opportunity to meet and observe other families who were also in the waiting room under similar circumstances.

There were two kinds of people in that waiting room. The first kind: the people who had faith in God and knew that their ailing loved one also had that same faith. They were secure in knowing that their loved one would go to a far better place if they did not survive. These families shared their concern, but they also shared a common love in the hope they had for the eternal condition of their loved one, should they not survive. These families, although very sad, were not bitter, and you could see the power of the hope they had in the way they spoke and loved each other.

The other people in that waiting room were those who did not have a faith in God, and their perspective and countenance were very different. In other words, they had no hope about the condition of their ailing loved one after death. It impacted their entire grieving experience. Many of them were very bitter, and their tears were based not in love but in anger and resentment. The contrast between the families with spiritual hope and those without was striking and very obvious. I have read and heard that hospice workers have experienced the same contrasting attitudes of the families they serve in the last days of life of a family member. This kind of hope is spiritual and heavenly, but we also have earthly hope that has the same kind of effect on our thinking and our attitude. People who have hope think differently and act differently.

I shared this story of Suzan's death for the purpose of illustrating just how powerful hope can be and how it can transform your attitude. If you can find hope, even in the darkest of events, your attitude will be better, and if your attitude is better, chances are you will perform better and have a superior chance for success. This is a basic truth about the human condition.

Hope is the reason some people do well in bad economic times and others fall into disastrous conditions. Hope is the reason that a person who has lost their job gets up every day and works hard to find another job. Hope is the reason a parent perseveres in training a troubled child and is willing to invest the time it takes to shape them into a responsible adult. Hope is the engine of your attitude, and your attitude determines your altitude.

ENCOURAGEMENT CREATES HOPE

The power of hope is incredible, but how can hope be created where there seems to be none? The answer is that hope springs from the kind of encouragement that helps you believe there is an opportunity for something better to happen. Amazingly, the kind of encouragement I'm talking about can be very simple, and sometimes it can come from a single principle or phrase—if the principle or phrase is what I call "self-evidently true." Self-evident truths are based on common sense, and when you hear one, you just know it is true—it requires no proof or justification to convince you. This kind of truth can be quite profound and may produce one of those "aha" moments of life that can be transforming in its effect.

> HOPE IS THE ENGINE OF YOUR ATTITUDE, AND YOUR ATTITUDE DETERMINES YOUR ALTITUDE.

I've had many of those aha moments in my own life, and I'll bet you have, too. The thousands of letters I have received through the years are almost identical in what they say.

Typically, people will write and tell me that at some point in their lives they were down on their luck and their lives and they had reached the end of their hope for the future. Then they say they either heard me speak, listened to my tapes, or read something in one of my books that had a powerful impact on their thinking and their lives. The letters always point to a single concept or thought that impacted them in a powerful, transforming way. The thing the ideas had in common was that they spoke to these people in their current condition, and they related to it. They found encouragement and hope in what they heard me say. Following are just a few of my quotes people have told me helped them develop hope and put them on the path of better thinking:

Failure is a detour, not a dead-end street.

You can have everything in life you want if you will just help enough other people get what they want.

It's not what you've got, it's what you use that makes a difference.

Remember that failure is an event, not a person.

You are the only person on earth who can use your ability. If you learn from defeat, you haven't really lost.

Success is not a destination, it's a journey.

Those who wait until all the lights are on green before starting will never leave home.

It's your attitude, not your aptitude, that determines your altitude.

All of these quotes and principles represent simple ideas that are self-evidently true and easily believed. The positive result of believing any of them and applying the principle in your daily life is hope. Hope gives you the ability to open your eyes and ears to the world around you and helps you become a recognizer of new opportunity.

RECOGNIZING NEW OPPORTUNITY

People with hope are constantly looking for the

opportunity in every situation. Those without hope are looking for the reason any opportunity won't work. Guess what either person finds?

As we established earlier, learning to become a good recognizer of new opportunities is a specific skill you need to develop to keep moving down the path to success. I have compared hope to a fuel and said it is the fuel that runs your attitude engine, and it is true. But your hope tank can be slowly drained over time, and it must be replenished by encouragement and the discovery of opportunity. This encouragement doesn't have to come from someone else. You can encourage yourself. Look in the mirror each day, put your shoulders back, and say, "Today is my day, there's opportunity everywhere, and I'm going to take advantage of every situation." Show me someone who never sees a new opportunity and I'll show you someone whose hope tank is being depleted or may even be empty. When I hear someone say, *"There is nothing I can do to* (fill in the blank)," I know it is being said by a person who does not know how to recognize opportunities and whose hope tank is low. I'm not saying that people don't experience tough times and that during those times things don't become more difficult. I'm talking about the problem of thinking, *"There is nothing I can do!"*

My fellow speaker, the late Earl Nightingale, told the story of an alcoholic father who had two sons. One son became an alcoholic and reasoned, "With a father like that, what else could I have done?" The other son made a commitment never to drink alcohol and went on to have a highly successful career and family life. "With a father like that," he reasoned, "what else could I have done?"

I have another question for you to consider. Do you believe there is something you can do right now that would make your life much worse? I'm sure you can think of several things. Well, if you can do something to make your life worse, you can do something right now to make your life better. You can keep doing the same things and you'll keep getting the same results. For every action you take, there is a result that follows. So take a different action and new opportunities will appear.

I believe "the immigrant attitude" is the best example I have of recognizing opportunity, and it has to do with belief. Have you ever wondered why there exists such a long list of people who want to enter America? It's because immigrants believe there is unlimited opportunity for them in America and they can pursue their dreams here. Many of them come to America from countries where opportunity is really in short supply—or non-existent—and they know the difference. When they come to America, they see beauty and opportunity everywhere—beyond their ability to imagine. They are amazed by the sheer number of jobs advertised in the papers. They understand many of them are "minimum wage" jobs, but those jobs are better than they could have ever obtained in their home country. They are willing to live as cheaply as possible and save their money so they can afford to invest in their education or a new business. A very high percentage of legal immigrants become self-employed. Amazingly, before they discover the problems and challenges other Americans gripe about, they are already a great success! They discovered how tough it was too late. All they could see when they arrived was the ability to live, work, and grow in the world's greatest country. That is the immigrant attitude, and it is the attitude you need to embrace, too.

Once you become a true believer that opportunity exists, the next thing you need to do is open your eyes and ears and soak up everything that is going on around you. I have found that avoiding negative people and associating with people who have been successful is the best way to recognize new opportunity. I've had many friends and a few family members through the years who have struggled with addiction issues. I have seen them recover and permanently kick the addiction issue that held them. One of the most powerful solutions they found was participating in some kind of recovery group and learning from others who had also overcome the same addiction. What they found in those groups was success and a positive hope that their lives could be changed and they could be happy without participating in their addiction. They associated with people who could give them practical advice and the daily tools they needed to be successful in their recovery. They also were given insight into opportunities that existed for them when they believed they had none.

Opportunity is walking through your life every day in the form of people you meet. Avoid reading their minds and pre-judging them. Every person you meet represents the possibility of discovering a new opportunity. For those people to show you that opportunity, you must listen and learn from them. Every success I've had in my life has begun by asking someone to teach me and help me do what I needed to do. I am not a mind reader. I listen to others who have been successful and evaluate their words. If what they say makes sense, then I follow their advice. It is from people and their success that I have been encouraged and given hope. Out of that encouragement and hope, I have always been able to find opportunity. You can do the same, and when you have that kind of hope and the ability to recognize new opportunities, you can certainly expect to win!

THERE IS HOPE IN THE FUTURE

Dr. John Maxwell says that if there's hope in the future, there is power in the present. The reason is simple: if there is hope in the future, that has a dramatic impact on your thinking today. Your thinking today determines your performance today, and your performance today has a direct bearing on your future.

CHAPTER ELEVEN

DON'T WORRY ABOUT RESULTS

Have you ever watched people bowl? Many of them go through a little ritual before they actually get to the point of hurling their bowling ball in the direction of the pins. They carefully lace up their bowling shoes, and then the hunt for the perfect bowling ball begins. They may put on a bowling glove as well as an elbow brace. As they step to the line they glare at the bowling pins and get into their approach posture. Then they step forward and release the bowling ball down the alley. That's when it gets interesting. As the ball rolls toward the pins the bowler starts deploying facial expressions, body language, and hand signals to "guide" the ball into the best impact point on the pins. As they see the ball drifting into a less-than-perfect point of impact they begin to give voice commands to the ball to correct its course. Of course, once the ball is released it is on the way, and there is nothing the bowler can do to change what is going to happen. The bowler could just as easily release the ball, turn around, and not even look at the impact of ball and pins. The results would be the same.

The bowling illustration demonstrates the futility of "worrying" about results. When you have set your goals properly and planned the action you need to take, as I have suggested in this book, it's a waste of time, energy, and emotion to worry about the results of what you have set in motion. When you execute an action step, it is like releasing a bowling ball. The results ball is rolling, and there is little you can do to change the point of impact. Worrying about where the ball will impact the target won't improve or change what happens. The results will be the fruit of how well you prepared and planned and executed the action.

WORRYING MAKES PROBLEMS WORSE

Worrying about the results will not change them.

I certainly recognize that a certain amount of worry is just part of being human. People have concerns about many things. There are legitimate concerns about money and financial security. There are legitimate concerns about health issues, and there are concerns about our personal and professional relationships. People want all of these things to go well in their lives, and a certain amount of worry and concern is normal. But there is another kind of worry that is not only dangerous to your health, it is dangerous to your success. The kind of worry I'm talking about is "imagined worry." Imagined worry is when you spend a lot of time thinking about the future and what might happen in your life that could be terrible. My late friend Mary Crowley said, "Worry is a misuse of the imagination," and she hit the nail on the head with that remark.

Now you might be wondering why I'm so concerned about worrying and what it has to do with success and expecting to win, so I'll tell you. Worry is the most significant factor that relates to the root of negative thinking. As a matter of fact, worry just might be the engine that starts negative thinking, and if you are involved in negative thinking, you will not expect to win. If you spend an excessive amount of time imagining all the bad things that can happen in your life, you will become a person who is problem-conscious, not solution-conscious. There is perhaps no greater example of how this can be so dangerous than when it involves worrying about health issues.

I have known many people who receive bad medical reports, and when they hear the news, they begin to worry so much about it their life may as well have ended at that moment. We all know people who suffer this way and we suffer with them. There doesn't seem to be a single thing we can do or say to encourage and lift them up.

On the other hand, we all know people who suffer in the worst way and never make mention of their struggle. In fact, they seem embarrassed if we catch them grimacing in pain or taking a bad step. They don't want attention focused on what they can't do or how they hurt and suffer; they want to be "others" centered and get their mind off of their disability. These individuals have accepted their issue as a part of life and have decided to make the very best of their circumstances. They are an encouragement and example to everyone blessed enough to know them! Yes, they have bad days, but they choose to focus on the good days and what they can still do. They live in the moment and know full well that tomorrow will be what it is and they can deal with it when it arrives, not before.

STOP WORRYING... START EXPECTING

Worry is the result of thinking and imagining what might happen in the future. I want to stress the word "imagine." The only reality people have is what is going on in their lives today. It is in the events of the day that life transpires, and anything based on tomorrow is pure speculation. I've learned that if you have planned and prepared, you *can* have reasonable expectations about the future. If you take care of your health through a good diet coupled with exercise, you can reasonably expect good health in the future. If you save and invest your financial resources, you can reasonably expect to have financial security in the future. If you live by principles of love and service to others, you can reasonably expect to have good personal relationships in the future. Good action today will produce good living tomorrow. Reasonably good expectations for tomorrow are based on positive thinking and prudent action today. Try this: instead of imagining all the bad things that might happen to you in the future based on your fear, start imagining things working out. There's a song titled, "What If It All Goes Right?" by Melissa Lawson. The second line of the chorus is, "What if it all works out, what if the stars all line up... " You have to develop a *what if it does go right and work out* expectancy if you want to be the winner you were born to be.

LIVING WITH EXPECTANCY

Throughout my career I have shared the story of Bernie Lofchick and his son, David. Bernie has been a lifelong friend, and we have been so close I refer to him as my brother even though we are not related. When David Lofchick was born, he was diagnosed with cerebral palsy, and doctors predicted he would be chronically crippled his entire life.

The only thing wrong with their prediction is that they did not know the positive optimism of David's father (my brother Bern). The Lofchicks did not throw up their hands and accept the idea that their son had no hope of a normal life. They did not worry and begin to imagine all the bad things that could result from David's disease. They immediately began to look for solutions and positive alternatives that would give David a good life. After many consultations with experts on David's disease, they found one doctor who gave them some positive hope for David's future. That doctor told them if they would begin a rigorous, daily exercise regimen for David, and consistently maintain that exercise program, his life might be saved from the gloomy forecast predicted for him.

Bernie and his family took the doctor 's advice, set up a gym in their home, and hired a physical therapist to provide the type of exercise David needed. The daily regime began so David's body could learn what it needed to know to make all of his tomorrows better. As David grew into a man, he continued on his own to follow the daily exercise routine prescribed for him. It had been predicted by most of his early doctors that David would never be able to walk, or talk, or count to ten. However, because his parents refused to worry about all the bad things that might happen to David and found things they could do to give David a different future, his life was changed. David certainly learned to walk and talk and count to ten. He also grew up to become a successful businessman, a wonderful father, and a reasonable golfer, capable of shooting a score in the eighties. All of this happened because his parents refused to worry and did what they needed to do each day to produce the positive results they wanted for David's future. They did not worry about the results. They just did what they knew they had to do and expected good things to happen.

As I stated earlier, worry is the engine of negative thinking. Once you start imagining all the bad things that may possibly happen in the future, you lose sight of the good things going on around you today! When alcoholics and drug-addicted people enter a program of recovery, one of the main things they must learn and begin to practice is the need to take each day as it comes and "live in the now." It is when addicted people learn this simple skill that their lives begin to change. They learn that most of their thinking and worrying about the future are imagined, and their imagination produces a tremendous amount of fear in their lives. The fear produced by worry is described as "**F**alse **E**vidence **A**ppearing **R**eal." When your thought life becomes dominated by imagining the disasters that may befall you in the future, you become a person without hope today.

The truth is that worrying creates extreme physical stress on your body. As a matter of fact, worry actually causes your body to generate hormones that create real anxiety. And it all comes from sitting around thinking about all the things that went wrong, are wrong, or could go wrong. A great solution for this condition (if you find yourself in it) is to get up out of your worry chair and do something. Many times just moving around will take your mind off some persistent, negative thought and help you correct your thinking. Do some laundry, call a friend, go for a long walk, or engage in some other form of physical exercise. The important thing, as my friend Andy Andrews says, "is to just *do* something!"

Did you know that indecision is also one of the main causes of worry? When you are unclear about taking a specific action, you are constantly tempted to think about the problem or challenge you may be facing, and that's when you begin to imagine all the bad things that can happen. The solution to this situation is to do the planning and preparation you need to do to make a decision. Don't be afraid of making a wrong decision, either. Once you make a decision you can stop worrying about the problem and move ahead. Winston Churchill said, "I never worry about action, but only inaction." Harry Truman said, "*Once a decision was made*, I did not *worry* about it afterward" (emphasis mine). Even if the results of your decision turn out to be less than you hoped for, you will learn from your mistake and be able to make a better decision next time.

Another source of worry you will want to avoid is what I call "perfectionistic thinking."Many people think if they are not perfect they will be considered a failure. This kind of attitude makes it difficult for a person to experience the normal setbacks in life and walk through them. An example would be that just because you failed to get a particular job or position, you develop the attitude that you will never get a job or a position. Remember, failure is an event, not a person.

In his book *I Can't Accept Not Trying: Michael Jordan on the Pursuit of Excellence*, Michael said, "I've missed more than 9,000 shots in my career. I've lost almost 300 games. Twenty-six times, I've been trusted to take the game-winning shot and missed. I've failed over and over and over again in my life. And that is why I succeed."

My granddaughter DeDe Galindo, a talented speaker if I do say so myself, bases her talk on a philosophy she calls "The Power of Next." DeDe says if you attempt something and you fail, you can always count on pulling yourself back up with the power of what you are going to do next. It's the next opportunity that keeps us motivated.

Mind reading also creates unnecessary worry about personal and professional relationships. If you are a reasonable student of human nature, you might be able to anticipate what people will do in specific situations. However, that is not mind reading. Mind reading is when you believe you can accurately discern another person's motive and intent based on something they *may* be thinking. Your relationships with others should be based on what they actually *do*, rather than what you believe they may be thinking! When you start reading people's minds, you are setting yourself up for a lot of worry and unnecessary concern.

The solution to a potentially bad relationship is to have a direct, open, honest conversation with whoever is involved. Remember, mind reading opens the door to unfounded speculation about the motives and intentions of others. And chances are you will be wrong. Mind reading is a great waste of time and energy and something you should avoid at all costs. It's better to confront a situation peacefully and directly. The truth is seldom as awful as imagined.

I DON'T WORRY

Worrying is something I quit doing many years ago, and today I can honestly tell you that I don't worry about anything—period! In fact, when the terrorist attack happened on 9/11 and I had to find a way to travel back home, I did not worry about the possibility of another attack. I believe if it is not my time, there's not a terrorist on the earth who can change the will of God about what my lifespan should be. I never worry because I know who I am and I know *Whose* I am. I know that the principles I live by are true and correct. I also know that I always try to do the right thing, and when you do the right things in life, you don't have to worry about results. As a matter of fact, if I've done the right thing every day I'm not even responsible for results. I just get the benefit of what I do, and the benefits are usually better than I could have hoped for.

Finally, remember that if you have planned and prepared yourself to win, there is no need to worry about the results. Like the bowler who has released the ball down the alley, you must learn there is nothing your worrying can do to change anything. If you have planned well and set good goals, you can have confidence that you know where you want and need to go. If you have done what you need to do to prepare yourself to win, you do not have to worry. You will have no justification to worry about failure. You can expect to win!

CHAPTER TWELVE

ALWAYS EXPECT THE BEST— BE A POSITIVE THINKER

Throughout my career I have heard people make less than complimentary remarks about the long-term impact of motivational messages and positive thinking. They say, "It's a waste of time and money because it doesn't last." They say, "People might be charged up temporarily, but they always drift back into their old habits and ways." People who make these kinds of remarks don't understand the power of thinking positively and what it takes to maintain a positive attitude and become the winner they were born to be.

I've frequently said that motivation is not permanent, but neither is bathing or eating! If you eat and bathe every day, you'll live longer and smell better in the process.

Some things just need to be done regularly! Or better yet, *all the time,* like I pointed out with Coach Vince Lombardi's quote about winning being an "all the time thing." Even winning is something you need to be motivated enough to do every day. Staying motivated enough to win is the only way I've found to achieve long-term winning results. Do we all backslide? Of course! Can you have a bad day? You bet! Is life going to knock you down? Sure it is. Are you going to

> POSITIVE THINKING WON'T ALLOW YOU TO DO ANYTHING, BUT IT WILL ALLOW YOU TO DO EVERYTHING BETTER THAN NEGATIVE THINKING WILL.

keep getting back up? Did you just hesitate? Like I said earlier, I'll help you with the hard ones. Of course you're going to get back up!

CHOOSE POSITIVE THINKING

Positive thinking won't allow you to do anything, but it will allow you to do *everything* better than negative thinking will. Doesn't that make sense? Sports provides some of the best illustrations to support this idea. What would you think of a sports team where the players were convinced of defeat before the game even began? What if the players sat around thinking and talking about how much bigger, faster, and more talented their opponent was and that they just didn't have even a hope of winning? What if the coach said, "Well, I don't even know why I'm asking you people to show up for this game, because they are just going to whip us all over the field!" If this were the attitude of the coach and the team, they wouldn't stand a chance of winning the game. They would live down to their own expectations.

When a person or a team or a business is characterized by negative thinking, they will always live down to their negative expectations. Positive thinking, on the other hand, will lift them to higher levels as they live *up* to their positive expectations.

So if positive thinking is the best way to go, why don't more people pursue a positive attitude? Why don't more businesses and organizations invest more money in helping their teams learn to think positively and get better results?

Here's the answer: positive thinking and what it takes to remain positive are misunderstood.

At the beginning of this book I said, *"You were born to win, but to be the winner you were born to be, you have to plan to win and prepare to win. Then and only then can you expect to win!"* In that statement you will find the complete formula that will take you to the top. And repeated daily throughout your life, it will keep you there.

The preceding chapters have discussed the elements of planning, preparation, and positive expectation and how to approach each of those areas. It's really very simple. You plan your tomorrows by understanding the vision you have for success, and you set your goals to accomplish your vision. Then you prepare and equip yourself with the knowledge, support, and tools you need to execute your goals. When you have planned and prepared, you will earn the right to expect to win, and expecting to win means doing what it takes to recognize hope and opportunity, which will support a great, positive attitude about your life and how you live it.

YOU PLAN YOUR TOMORROWS BY UNDERSTANDING THE VISION YOU HAVE FOR SUCCESS, AND YOU SET YOUR GOALS TO ACCOMPLISH YOUR VISION.

IT'S ALL ABOUT PERFORMANCE

Much of success is about performance. It's about what we do and what we are able to inspire others to do. There are some simple performance principles I have learned in my life, and it's appropriate to wrap up *Born to Win* with a brief discussion of each. They really bring success, and what it takes to be successful, into sharp focus. They are also the basis for developing and maintaining an expectation of success.

The Six Principles of Performance

1. **We generally get from ourselves and others what we expect.** I made this point earlier, but it is a huge fact that you will either live up or down to your own expectations. If you expect to lose, you will. If you expect to be average, you will be average. If you expect to feel bad, you probably will. If you expect to feel great, nothing will slow you down. And what is true for you is true for others. Your expectations for others will become what they deliver and achieve. As Gandhi said, "Be the change you wish to see in the world."
2. **The difference between good and excellent companies is training.** The only thing worse than training employees and losing them is to not train them and keep them! A football team would not be very successful if they did not train, practice, and prepare for their opponents. When you think of training as practice and preparation, it makes you wonder how businesses survive that do not make significant training investments in their people.
3. **Actually, companies that do not train their people and invest in their ability don't last.** They operate from a competitive disadvantage and are eventually gobbled up and defeated in the marketplace. If you want to improve and move from good to excellent, a good training strategy will be the key to success.
4. **You find what you look for in life.** If you look for the good things in life, you will find them. If you look for opportunities to grow and prosper, you will find them. If you look for positive, enthusiastic friends and associates who will support you, you

will find them. On the other hand, if you look for ways to cheat, you will cheat. If you look for ways to justify leaving your spouse, you will find them. If you look for justifiable reasons to hold a grudge against another person, you will find those, too. It is a natural tendency of us all to look for things that will justify what we think we need or want. If you are not living by the foundation stones of honesty, character, integrity, faith, love, and loyalty, you will be drawn to seeking selfish gratification, and that leads to misery and unfulfilled dreams. Whatever you have will never be enough. Always look for the good and for ways to help others.

5. **Never make a promise without a plan.** Far too many people make promises they can never keep. They may have the best intentions in the world to keep their promise, but if they have not made a plan to keep it, they will not be able to do it. Business leaders who make promises to their employees will not honor them if they do not create a plan on how the promises will be kept. If you make a future commitment, you must understand and be willing to do whatever it takes to complete that commitment. One of the reasons marriage commitments fail so frequently is because the husband and wife do not understand what it takes to have a great marriage. They do not plan for or understand the sacrifices each must make for the other to enable a long-lasting relationship.
6. **Happiness, joy, and gratitude are universal if we know what to look for.** I believe you can have everything in life you want if you will just help enough other people get what they want. All people want happiness and joy in their life, but you have to know what produces real happiness and how

to do the things that produce it. The moment you begin to worry about the things you want and the things you don't have in life is the moment you will lose your gratitude for what you actually have. If you are ungrateful, you will never be satisfied or content or joyful about your life. The greatest source of happiness is the ability to be grateful at all times.

THE RIGHT ATTITUDE

Obviously, the right attitude to expect the best in your life is a positive attitude. But I want to be very clear that the kind of positive attitude I describe is not one that is contrived or falsely manufactured to impress or manipulate others. The positive attitude I talk about is one that you are filled with, and when you are jostled, it just spills out! What I'm saying is that a genuine positive attitude is part of who you are at your core.

If you have a bad attitude, it is a reflection of who you are, as well. It's a "heart condition," and to get rid of that bad attitude, you need a change of heart. I would be remiss if I did not acknowledge that God is the most amazing heart surgeon available to us all. He does not just repair a bad heart, He can give you a new one that your body will not reject. The new heart He provides will produce love, joy, peace, patience, kindness, goodness, faithfulness, gentleness, and self-control in your life. When you have those characteristics and qualities in your life, you will be rightfully positioned to know beyond a shadow of a doubt that you are truly *born to win*.

CHAPTER THIRTEEN
BORN TO WIN FOR BUSINESS LEADERS

One of the reasons I love the *Born to Win* concepts we are covering is that they perfectly tie together your personal life and your business life. It doesn't matter if you are a business owner, a sales professional, a corporate executive or a team member, you can use these principles to plan, prepare, expect, and achieve success in your business life while at the same time creating a fulfilling personal life. To achieve balanced success, everything you do must support everything else you do, and your daily actions must propel you toward your life vision and goals.

My good friend Howard Partridge has a powerful quote that connects your business life to your personal life. "Your business exists for one reason and one reason only – as a vehicle to help you achieve your life goals."

If you are not a business owner you can easily substitute "your career" for "your business" to fully understand the impact of this statement. At Ziglar we say we are really in the transportation business: *We help you get from where you are to where you want to be.* Question: Can you say without a doubt that your business or career is the vehicle that will allow you to achieve your life goals and take you to where

> "YOUR BUSINESS EXISTS FOR ONE REASON AND ONE REASON ONLY – AS A VEHICLE TO HELP YOU ACHIEVE YOUR LIFE GOALS."
> *HOWARD PARTRIDGE*

you want to be? Not sure? That's okay! In the next few pages I will show you a simple illustration that will bring together your personal life and your business life, so that you will know without a doubt what you need to do in order to create the vehicle that will allow you to achieve your vision and life goals.

If I am *born to win,* what is winning? Understanding this question is critical to establishing the right kind of life goals. Believe me, nothing is more frustrating than achieving the wrong goals! In Ziglar's forty-plus years of researching this, we have determined that there are eight things in life that everybody wants. No matter what your specific life goals are, you must also achieve these eight things in order to be truly successful.

Everybody wants to be:

- Happy
- Healthy
- Reasonably Prosperous and
- Secure

They want to have:

- Friends
- Peace of Mind
- Good Family Relationships and
- Hope

Once you understand that these are the eight things your life goals and vision must include, you can begin to work on the key areas in your personal life to achieve them. (We covered these earlier in the Wheel of Life.)

Happy
Healthy
Prosperous
Secure
Friends
Peace
Family
Hope

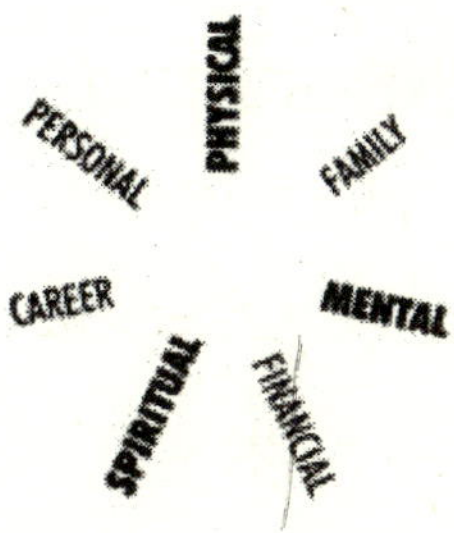

As you work on each spoke of your Wheel of Life, it is essential that you do everything with character. Character allows you to make the right choices in life when things are tough and when temptation comes. Nothing can crush your Wheel of Life faster than character failure. Character makes the toughest, bumpiest ride in life doable. Fred Smith, the toughest, bumpiest ride in life doable. Fred Smith, Dad's mentor and the wisest man I've ever met, said that every great failure in life is really a moral failure. When-ever you encounter someone who seemingly had everything and then lost it, it is almost always as a result of a character flaw and a moral issue. On the other hand, men and women who have great character and suffer a seemingly devastating fall from the world's definition of success, almost always seem to bounce back to a higher and more meaningful level of success. Why? As Willie Jolley says, their character allows them to use "the setback as a setup for a comeback." With character the eight things in life are probable; without character they are impossible.

Happy
Healthy
Prosperous
Secure
Friends
Peace
Family
Hope

CHARACTER

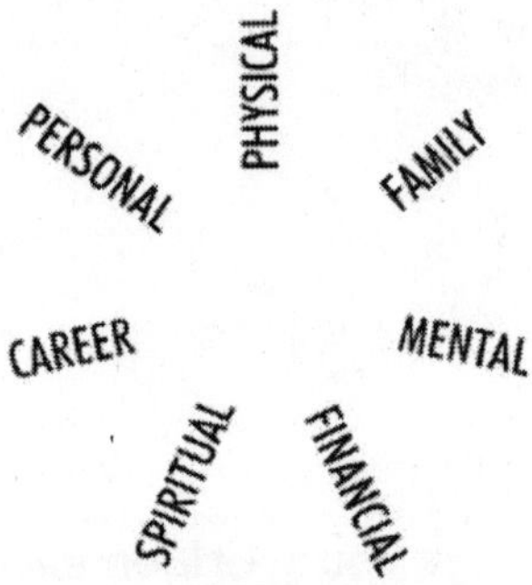

Working on your character and the spokes on your wheel to achieve the eight things in life everybody wants creates vision. The V in the diagram below stands for your vision. Without character and a balanced Wheel of Life, you are literally unable to focus on the eight things that really matter. You will not be able to tell the difference between a house and a home or a bed and a good night's sleep. In short, your vision is blurred because you are out of balance, without stability, and your lack of character fogs your view. Imagine standing on a small boat in very rough seas, looking through a telescope with the lenses fogged up. This is exactly what happens when you have an unbalanced Wheel of Life and an undeveloped weak character. It is, however, possible to have good character and an unbalanced Wheel of Life. When this happens you can see through the telescope clearly, but as the boat rocks back and forth you lose sight of the eight things! Great vision requires both a balanced Wheel of Life and character.

Happy
Healthy
Prosperous
Secure
Friends
Peace
Family
Hope

character

PHYSICAL
PERSONAL
FAMILY
CAREER
MENTAL
SPIRITUAL
FINANCIAL

Now you need some P.C.! P.C. stands for **persistent consistency**. I asked Dad while we were working on this book what he considered his biggest key to success other than character and integrity and he said persistent consistency was the number one reason for his success in life. Consistency means doing the things that you need to do in order to achieve success every single day. Persistency means sticking with it and doing the little extras so that every time you do it (consistency) you are getting better and better. An example would be how you get in great shape. You work out consistently (five days a week) with persistency (each time you work out you increase your weight, or your intensity, or add a new exercise). Another definition for P.C. is work ethic. Working hard is important. Working with P.C. is a true difference-maker.

Happy
Healthy
Prosperous
Secure
Friends
Peace
Family
Hope

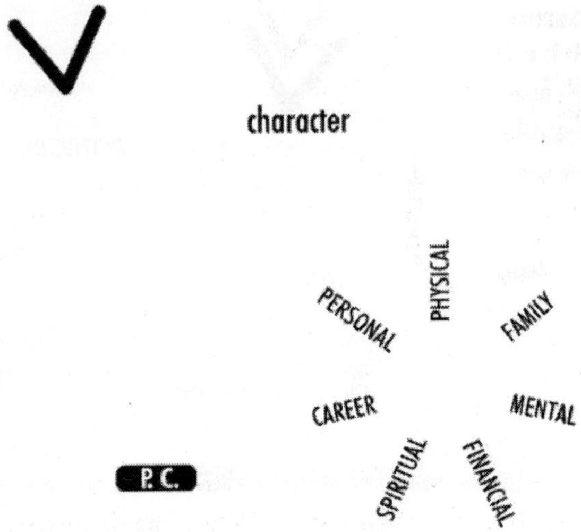

The Business/Career Connection

Just like you evaluated your personal Wheel of Life, you can also evaluate your Business/Career Wheel. For the purposes of this example, we are going to use a Business Wheel where you are the owner/operator of the business.

A Business Wheel has five major spokes:

- Marketing – how you bring prospects to the business
- Sales – how you convert prospects into customers
- Operations – how you service and support customers
- Administration – the systems, processes, procedures and financial aspects that make things run efficiently
- Leadership – the strategic goals, vision, planning, and staff development

Obviously, there are more elements to a successful business than listed here, but everything can fall under these five spokes.

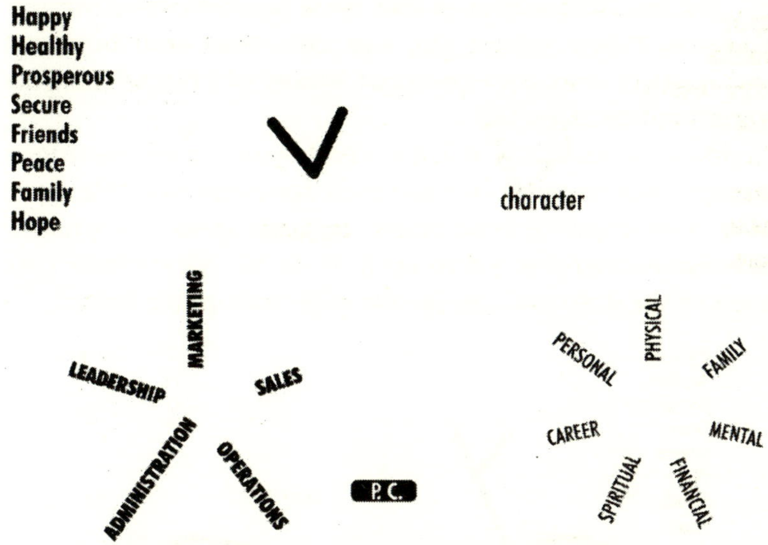

As in your personal Wheel of Life, you can also rate yourself in your Business Wheel to determine how smooth your ride is. The illustration below gives an example of how typical business operators may rate themselves on both wheels.

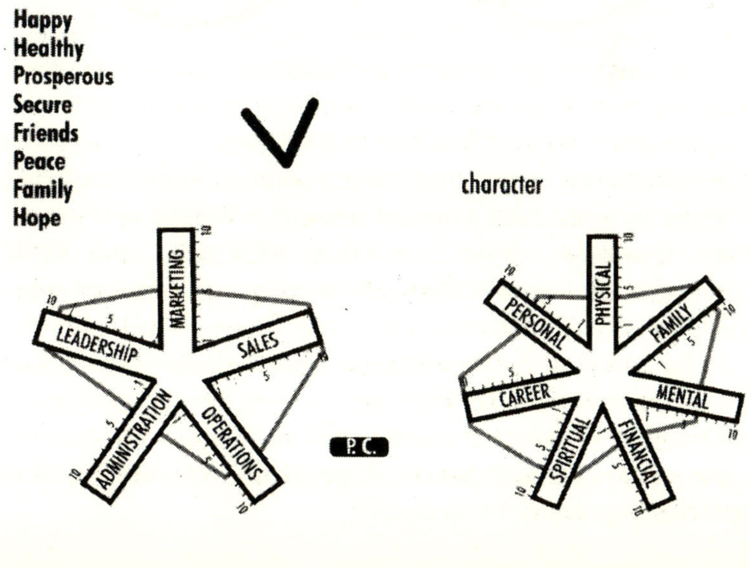

(In the Addendum of this book we provide a sample Business Wheel where you can rate your own business and connect it to your personal Wheel of Life, which you completed on page 46.)

Now, as you look at these wheels you can tell the ride is going to be bumpy as the rider rolls down the road! The goal now is to improve your rating on each spoke, eventually moving everything out to an 8, 9, or 10. Now when you connect the dots you can see the rider rolls much better!

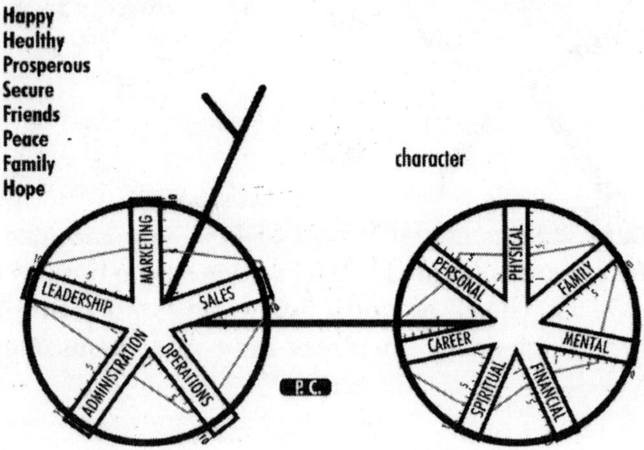

The only way to achieve balanced success in your business and your personal life is to connect all of the components. Your Business Wheel and your personal Wheel of Life are connected. Your vision must be supported by both wheels. Don't forget Howard Partridge's quote: **"Your business exists for ONE REASON and ONE reason ONLY – as a VEHICLE to help you achieve your Life Goals."**

Character is the foundation upon which you sit that gives you sustainable leverage as you apply persistent consistency. Character allows you to handle the bumps in the road so much better. It provides the cushion that separates you from the seatpost!

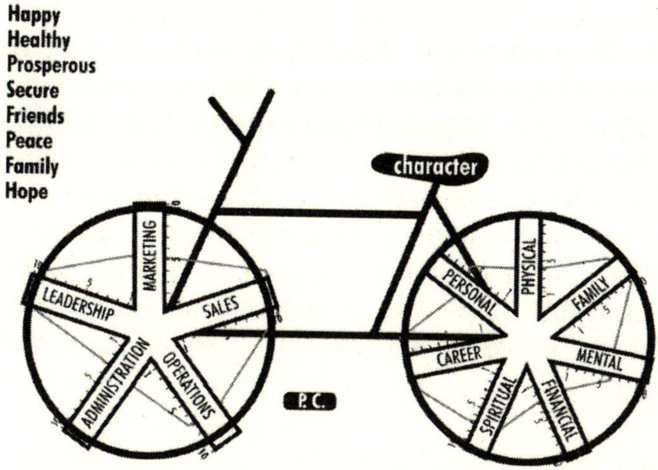

Now we have a vehicle that is almost ready to roll. If you start pedaling this bike down the road, it's not going anywhere just yet! It needs a chain. Goals are the links in the chain that connect activity to accomplishment. As you work on each spoke of your wheels, you will determine and set specific goals. As you apply P.C. to each goal, this chain of energy will move your bike! As long-time Ziglar sales professional Michael McGowan says, P.C. really stands for Pedaling like Crazy!

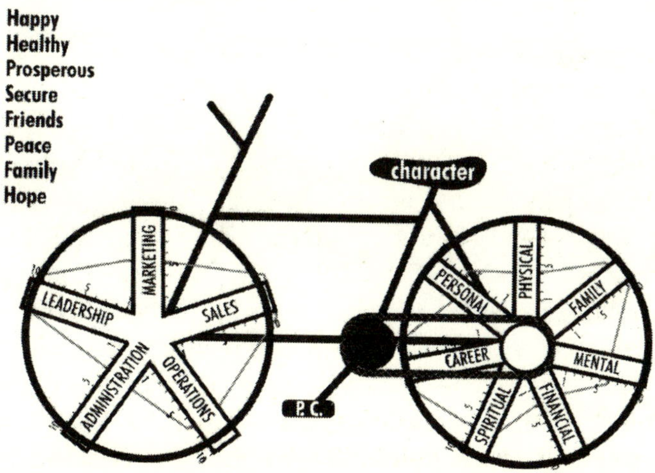

If you are like me, not only do you want to win but you want to win faster, and you want to win more easily. This is where gears come in. Don't settle for a one-speed bike when you can just as easily have a 10-speed, or even a 20-speed bike. Gears are simply the outside resources of knowledge and support that you need to go faster and to keep you going when you have tough hills to climb. Gears include things like books, CDs, online learning, coaching, seminars, and professional development training. In my experience, nothing keeps your bike moving forward on a daily basis better than listening to personal and professional development audio programs every day. If you are experiencing frustration in your current situation or want to take your business and personal life to the next level of success, you seriously need to consider adding the gear of coaching.

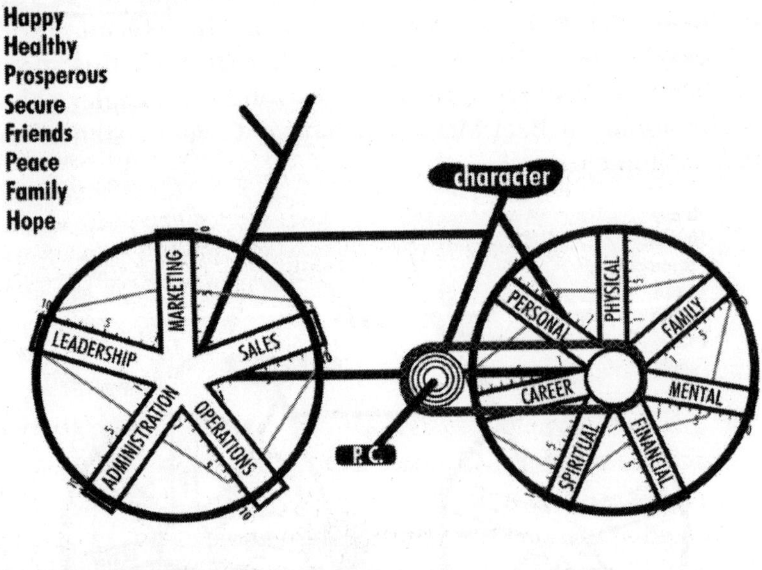

Dad's Secret

Through the years, many people have asked me, "What

has allowed your dad to achieve so much success and to sustain it for so long?" My answer includes everything pictured in this diagram, plus one more element. Years ago, when Dad was forty-five years old, he changed his gear ratio and added a "super charger" to his bike. That is when he became a Christian and made God the center hub of his Wheel of Life and Wheel of Business. This became Dad's "why" and gave him fuel and wisdom far beyond his own to keep on pedaling. In order to go as far as you want to go in life—and for me I want to ride into eternity—I challenge you to consider your why in life. When you find the answer you will discover, just like I have, that it makes the ride incredibly amazing and worthwhile!

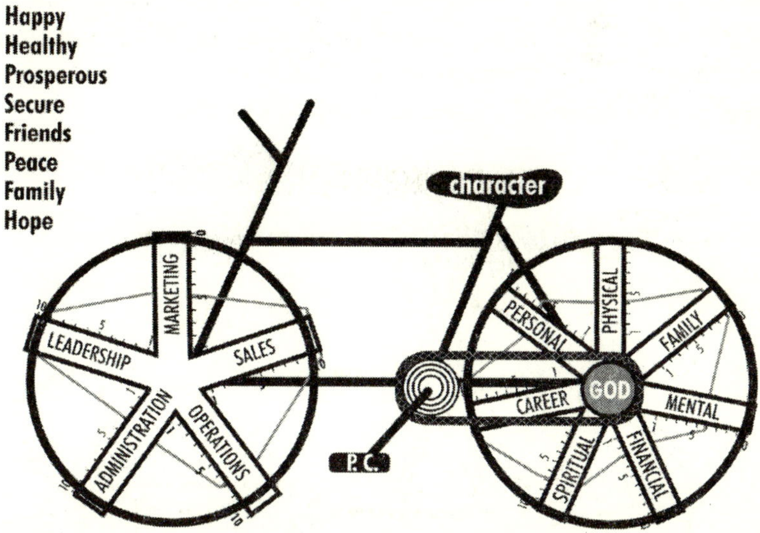

I want to share with you an "inside funny" between Dad and me. Several times in my life I have come up with an idea or thought that was pretty good, and Dad has looked at me and with humor in his voice said, "You're just not that smart!" Of course, I have said the same thing to him on several occasions after he has had one of his brilliant thoughts or concepts. The "inside funny" is this. We both realize we are not that smart! That idea came out of the hub! It's Dad's secret. I work on my hub every day, and I encourage you to do the same thing. I can prove it's true as well. Dad created a mathematical formula that proves it: YOU + God = Enough

My attitude about our company (you know I believe without a doubt that I was born to win – after all, it's part of my genes!) is so positive that our mission statement is to make a positive difference in the personal, family, business, and spiritual lives of enough people to make a positive difference in the world! Make it your mission right now, at this very moment, to make enough positive changes in your personal, family, business, and spiritual life that you can ultimately make a difference in the world! Change starts with you, but it doesn't start until you do. What are you waiting for? Go! Prepare yourself! Expect success! Change the world! After all... you are *BORN TO WIN*!

HOW SMOOTH IS YOUR RIDE?

TAKE THE FREE ZIGLAR TRUE PERFORMANCE PERSONALITY ASSESSMENT

We each have our own Wheel of Life, but all of our wheels are not the same. Do you have thriving friendships but struggle financially? Or perhaps you are excelling quickly in your career, but your poor physical condition sometimes makes it hard to get up in the morning. These are examples of an unbalanced wheel. While everyone will experience fluctuations in their wheel from time to time, the ideal wheel is balanced, creating a smooth journey through life. The first step to creating balance is to find out where you are right now!

Ziglar has developed a short, *free* assessment so that you can see which areas of your wheel need a little pumping up. In just five minutes or less you will:

- Rate yourself in the seven key areas of life
- See your wheel as it is *now*
- Learn how to get where you want to go—*faster*

By identifying where you are and setting the goals for where you want to be, you can achieve a healthy, happy, balanced life.

Simply go to www.ziglar.com/borntowin and see an *actual* depiction of your wheel!

ADDENDUM

PUTTING IT ALL TOGETHER – BUILD YOUR OWN BIKE

Is your business the vehicle that is allowing you to achieve your life's goals? If not, or you're not sure, let's figure it out and do an assessment on your Business Wheel. As a business owner/operator, your business has five key components or spokes.

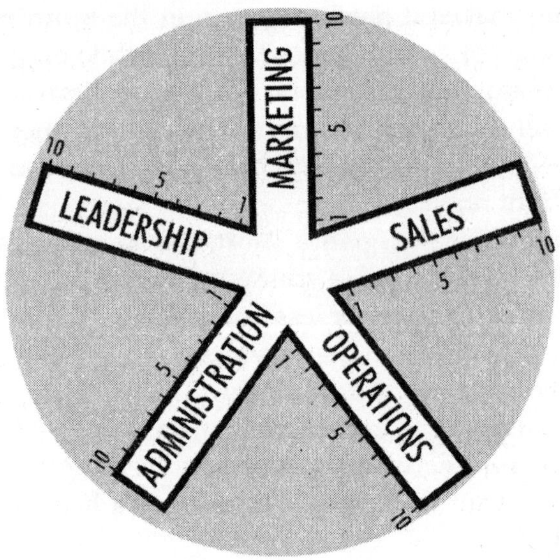

What is your rating for each one of the spokes? To find out, rate yourself on a scale of 1 to 10 for each item listed under each category on the following pages. When you have done that, add up your total score for that category and divide by 10. That will give you your rating on that spoke. Then, mark the numbers on your spokes and connect the dots. This will tell you where you need to improve and how smoothly your business is rolling down the road!

BUSINESS WHEEL
Category Assessment Sheet

Marketing

______ Meeting or exceeding my sales goals through effective lead generation and promotion strategies

______ We have a clear position in the marketplace

______ We have clearly defined our prime target market

______ We have clear definitions of our products and/or services

______ We have a pricing strategy that is profitable

______ We are consistently marketing to our house list (client base)

______ We have an effective referral relationship program

______ We have an effective referral/affiliate reward system

______ We have a written, posted marketing calendar

______ We have an effective Internet marketing system that includes websites that clearly communicate what we do, and utilize SEO, and we are consistently capturing e-mail addresses and using them to communicate to our e-mail audience, and we have a strong presence on social media.

______ TOTAL ÷ 10 = ________________

Sales

______ We answer the telephone live

______ We have an effective telephone answering/transferring system

______ We have an effective sales script that appeals to our target market and closes the maximum number of inquiries

______ We have an effective system for responding to Internet leads

______ We have an effective sales process for each of our profit centers

______ We have an effective up-sell and down-sell process

______ We have effective processes and scripts for overcoming objections

______ We have an effective process for identifying ongoing and changing customer needs

______ We have clearly defined account management policies and procedures

______ We have effective customer management software in place

______ TOTAL ÷ 10 = ______________

Operations

______ We have developed our unique service experience

______ We have clear-cut service systems in place that are exceeding our client expectations

______ We respond immediately to client concerns

______ We have clear-cut return policies

______ We get customer feedback on a regular basis to ensure we are exceeding expectations

______ We have regular production meetings to ensure on-time delivery

______ We have a key customer appreciation process

______ We have effective project management processes in place

______ We have inventory management and office supplies/ equipment processes in place

______ We have the latest, most effective equipment to

deliver our unique service experience
______ TOTAL ÷ 10 = ________________

Administration

______ We track and report total sales daily
______ We track and report sales by profit center weekly, monthly and annually
______ We track and report sales by referral/affiliate/ad source weekly
______ We track and report sales closings daily (# of calls vs. # of sales)
______ We track and report number of returns or re-services as often as they occur
______ We track and report our profit and loss weekly
______ We track and report our balance sheet monthly
______ We have a cash flow management process in place
______ We plan our taxes annually before year end
______ We review our legal and insurance exposure annually (or as often as required)
______ TOTAL ÷ 10 = ________________

Leadership

______ We have a one-sentence mission statement that everyone understands and follows
______ We have effective management systems in place that include recruiting, hiring, orientation, training, coaching, employee reviews and termination processes, and have ensured they are legal
______ We have an up-to-date employee handbook
______ We have a written business plan that includes our vision, goals, a marketing plan, sales plan, operating plan and administration plan that is reviewed and updated quarterly
______ We have a written and posted organizational chart

______ We have regular team meetings
______ We have written position descriptions for every position
______ We have a training system in place for every position
______ We have policies and procedures for all areas of our business
______ We have an effective compensation plan in place that includes attractive pay and benefits that create high employee morale and retention
______ TOTAL ÷ 10 = ________________

Now that you have completed your Business Wheel, let's take a look at your bike. Connect the dots on each of the wheels below using your score from above for the Business Wheel and your scores from page 46 on your Personal Wheel of Life.

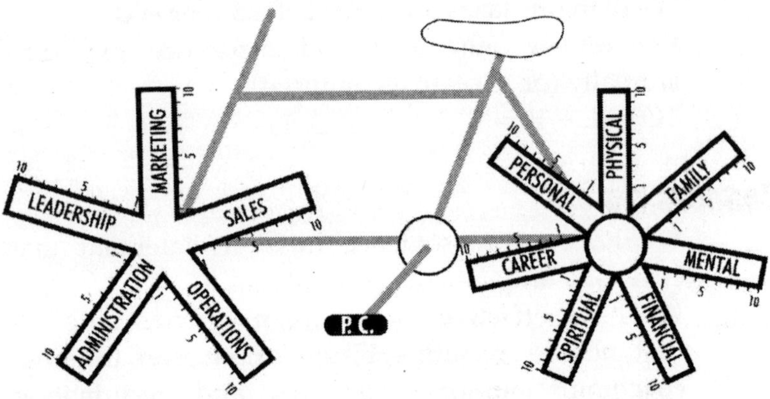

Now that you can see YOUR BIKE, you have a great place to start planning your goals. Look at your spokes and determine which ones you want to start working on. Once you have identified one, you can turn that into a goal using the Ziglar Goal Setting System in the next section.

Would you like more information on how to make your business the vehicle that allows you to achieve your life's goals? (Call us at 1.800.527.0306 and ask about Ziglar Business Coaching!)

The Ziglar Goal Setting System; "Goals are the links in the chain that connect Activity to Accomplishment."

—Tom Ziglar

THE ZIGLAR GOAL SETTING SYSTEM

GOAL PLANNING SHEETS AND STEP-BY-STEP PROCEDURES FOR SETTING AND REACHING YOUR GOALS

The Chinese say that the journey of a thousand leagues begins with a single step. Commit yourself to take these goal-setting steps NOW.

BAD NEWS: To properly set your goals you will need to invest a minimum of ten hours and possibly as many as twenty hours. That's one of the reasons only 3% of the population have clearly defined their objectives in life.

GOOD NEWS: By following these procedures and working on your goals every day, you will have **several** extra hours each week to pursue your own business, family and personal interests. Just remember, "When you do the things you need to do, when you need to do them, the day will come when you can do the things you want to do, when you want to do them."

MORE GOOD NEWS: When you learn the formula for setting one goal, you will know how to set all goals, whether it is a physical, mental, spiritual, social, family, career, recreational or financial goal.

Now for the action steps:

ACTION STEP I

On your Dream List, let your imagination run wild and print everything you want to be, do or have. (When you **print**, your concentration is greater and you burn the idea more indelibly into your subconscious mind.) If you have a family, be sure to include your mate and children when you set your goals. This entire goal-setting process helps channel your logical left brain and frees your creative right brain for more effective use of your imagination. NOTE: "You gotta **'be'** before you can **'do'**, and you gotta 'do' before you can **'have'**."

GO AHEAD – DO IT NOW. A major reason you are setting your goals is to gain some benefit, but these come only after you have taken action.

ACTION STEP II

Wait 24-48 hours then answer the question "why?" for each item you have printed on your Dream List. Space is provided for you to do this on your Things I Really Want To Be, Do or Have sheet. If you can't verbalize in one sentence why you want to "be, do or have," then it truly is a dream and not a real goal. At this point, you should cross it off your list.

ACTION STEP III

Ask these five questions, *all* of which must have a "yes" answer:

1. Is it really my goal? (If you're a minor living at home, an employee or a team member, some of your goals will be set by the coach, director, parent or employer.)

2. Is it morally right and fair to everyone concerned?
3. Is it consistent with my other goals?
4. Can I emotionally commit myself to finish this goal?
5. Can I "see" myself reaching this goal?

NOTE: Answering these questions will further reduce the number of dreams on your Things I Really Want To Be, Do or Have sheet, so scratch them off as well. Answering questions #2 and #3 will be very helpful in making important decisions in all areas of life, especially financial.

ACTION STEP IV

After each remaining dream ask yourself these questions:

1. Will reaching this goal make me happier?
2. Will reaching this goal make me healthier?
3. Will reaching this goal make me more prosperous?
4. Will reaching this goal win me more friends?
5. Will reaching this goal give me peace of mind?
6. Will reaching this goal make me more secure?
7. Will reaching this goal improve my relationships with others?

If you can't answer "yes" to at least one of these questions eliminate that item from your list of dreams. Careful: Don't confuse pleasure with happiness. Be sure to con-sider your family when you answer these questions.

ACTION STEP V

Divide the remaining goals into three categories: Short-range (1 month or less); Intermediate (1 month to 1 year);

Long-range (1 year or more), and mark them SR (short-range), I (intermediate) or LR (long-range) on your Things I Really Want To Be, Do or Have sheet. GO AHEAD – DO IT NOW. By taking this step you will be able to quickly determine whether or not you have a balanced perspective between what needs to be done now, versus your dreams for the future.

Remember:

1. SOME goals must be **big** (out of reach – not out of sight) to make you stretch and grow to your full potential.
2. SOME goals must be **long-range** to keep you on track and greatly reduce the possibility of short-range frustrations.
3. SOME goals must be small and **daily** to keep you disciplined and in touch with the reality of "nitty gritties" of daily life.
4. SOME goals must be **ongoing**.
5. SOME goals (sales, educational, financial, weight loss, etc.) might require **analysis and consultation** to deter-mine where you are before you can set the goals.
6. MOST goals should be **specific**. A "nice home" is not as good as "3,000 square foot, Tudor-style home with 4 bedrooms, 3 full baths, 2 living spaces," etc. Some goals, like improving your self-image, becoming a better parent or getting a better education, are more difficult to pinpoint. Those that are less specific should be broken down into specific, tangible steps. For instance, a step to becoming a better parent

could be "spend one hour per week one-on-one with each child."

ACTION STEP VI

From the remaining goals, prayerfully choose the four goals (remember, balance is the key) which are the most important things you need to work on **right now** and record them. If this is your first organized goal-setting experience, you may want to start with two or three short-range goals.

IMPORTANT: As you set a new goal, also record it in a journal or a place you will review several times a year. You will be encouraged tremendously as you record the goals you reach throughout the year. Your confidence, self-image and goals-achieving ability will improve dramatically.

ACTION STEP VII

Record these four goals (at least the ones that are Intermediate and Long-Range) on a General Goals Procedure Chart, and work each one of them through the process as shown in the examples.

ACTION STEP VIII

Take the additional goals you have listed on your Things I Really Want To Be, Do or Have sheet and record each on a General Goals Procedure Chart. Work each goal through the process as you did in Action Step VII. Refer to the examples for a format to follow.

DO IT NOW. Remember, motivation comes **after** you start the project.

CONGRATULATIONS! You have invested more time in planning your future than most of your friends, relatives and associates will ever invest!

DREAM LIST

EVERYTHING – I even *think* I want to be, do or have

THINGS I REALLY WANT TO BE, DO OR HAVE

After each item on your Dream List, articulate in one sentence **why**. This will eliminate those items which are frivolous whims but leave intact your serious goals and dreams.

Goals	*Why*

GENERAL GOALS PROCEDURE CHART	
Goal #1	Goal #2
Step #1 IDENTIFY YOUR GOALS	
Original Goal 165 lbs. – 34" waist	Get a "Better" Education
Step #2 MY BENEFITS FOR REACHING THIS GOAL	
More energy – less illness Look and feel better Longer life span Better endurance More productivity Better attitude and disposition More creativity Better example	Broaden and increase opportunities Improve self-image and increase relationships Increase income Improve security and knowledge Broaden personal, business and social life and contacts Improve discipline – peace of mind Increase happiness – confidence Enhance sense of accomplishment
Step #3 MAJOR OBSTACLES AND MOUNTAINS TO CLIMB TO REACH THIS GOAL	
Lack of discipline Bad weather – irregular schedule Love for sweets – lack of time Unhealthy eating habits Poor physical condition	Lack of patience – physical Exhaustion – financial costs Heavy family demands – lack of confidence (out of school 15-20 yrs.)
Step #4 SKILLS OR KNOWLEDGE REQUIRED TO REACH THIS GOAL	
Dieting knowledge and techniques Exercise and jogging procedures	Time management – positive attitude Patience – persistence – discipline Better money management Effective study procedures

Step #5 INDIVIDUALS, GROUPS, COMPANIES AND ORGANIZATIONS TO WORK WITH TO REACH THIS GOAL	
Dr. Ken Cooper, Dr. Randy Martin, Program Chairman – Laurie Magers, The Redhead	Family – employer – academic counselor – financial consultant – mentor
Step #6 PLAN OF ACTION TO REACH THIS GOAL	
Make commitment No bread or sweets except on Sunday Jog 125 minutes weekly Good breakfast – only fruit or healthy snacks after late seminars Eat well-balanced diet Drink 8 glasses of water daily Eat slowly and only at the table	Make commitment – organize time Practice self-discipline (cut TV time) Secure family support – schedule significant family time Listen to educational, inspirational recordings while driving Attend seminars Reduce meaningless activities Schedule study time daily Shape up physically for increased energy
Step #7 COMPLETION DATE	
July 1st	None – on-going goal

GENERAL GOALS PROCEDURE CHART	
Goal #1	Goal #2
Step #1 IDENTIFY YOUR GOALS	
Acquire a new black SUV with leather seats	Be a loving, attentive, involved parent
Step #2 MY BENEFITS FOR REACHING THIS GOAL	
More dependable transportation	More happiness and peace of mind

<table>
<tr><td>Raise my sights and standards
Improve job reliability
Better attitude
Increase travel opportunities
Enhance social status
Greater safety
More comfort and fun</td><td>More stable marriage
Better relationship with children, friends, neighbors and relatives
Better career opportunities
More old age security
Enjoyment of future grandchildren
Increase potential of children</td></tr>
<tr><td colspan="2">Step #3 MAJOR OBSTACLES AND MOUNTAINS TO CLIMB TO REACH THIS GOAL</td></tr>
<tr><td>Short of cash – Poor money management
Present car has low trade-in value
Income stabilized – inflation – mate disagrees
Higher payments and insurance costs</td><td>Limited experience – Tight budget
Heavy workload – Lack of patience
Inadequate help or no help
Alcoholic parent</td></tr>
<tr><td colspan="2">Step #4 SKILLS OR KNOWLEDGE REQUIRED TO REACH THIS GOAL</td></tr>
<tr><td>Money management – Automobile knowledge
Dollar stretching techniques
Information on how to buy and trade</td><td>Mental, nutritional, spiritual and physical information
Read books on common sense, diplomacy, communication skills, time management, organizational skills
Discipline
Know something about being a "fixer"</td></tr>
<tr><td colspan="2">Step #5 INDIVIDUALS, GROUPS, COMPANIES AND ORGANIZATIONS TO WORK WITH TO REACH THIS GOAL</td></tr>
<tr><td>Family – Banker/Financier – Insurance agent – Employer – Investment counselor – Part-time employer – Automobile dealer</td><td>Minister – Employer – Family physician – Mate – Youth leaders – Educators – Parents – In-laws Neighbors – Parent support groups</td></tr>
</table>

Step #6 PLAN OF ACTION TO REACH THIS GOAL	
Get financial statement Record expenditures for 30 days Skip vacation and deposit savings Follow ads and bargain hunt Establish and control budget Get family involved in their new vehicle Take family "window shopping" to see dream vehicle Deposit savings every week in interest-bearing accounts Take temporary and limited part-time job	Read books on positive parenting methods Assign daily responsibilities Provide daily mental and spiritual input and direction Spend time daily talking, directing, teaching and encouraging Accept and love my kids unconditionally Give them daily doses of affection and approval Expect, teach and require them to do their best Discipline properly and consistently Admit when wrong and ask for forgiveness
Step #7 COMPLETION DATE	
January 1st	Intangible

GENERAL GOALS PROCEDURE CHART	
Goal #1	Goal #2
Step #1 IDENTIFY YOUR GOALS	
Step #2 MY BENEFITS FOR REACHING THIS GOAL	

Step #3	MAJOR OBSTACLES AND MOUNTAINS TO CLIMB TO REACH THIS GOAL
Step #4	SKILLS OR KNOWLEDGE REQUIRED TO REACH THIS GOAL
Step #5	INDIVIDUALS, GROUPS, COMPANIES AND ORGANIZATIONS TO WORK WITH TO REACH THIS GOAL
Step #6	PLAN OF ACTION TO REACH THIS GOAL
Step #7	COMPLETION DATE

Plan your goals weekly and work on them daily! Ziglar has an incredible tool called the Performance Planner™ that helps you set, record and achieve your goals. You can learn more at www.ziglar.com.

REACHING YOUR GOALS
(To be *carefully* read at the end of *every* week.)

1. Make the commitment to reach your goal. "One person with a commitment is worth a hundred who only have an interest." **—Mary Crowley**
2. Commit yourself to detailed accountability. Record your weekly activities and list the six most important things, in the order of their importance, which you need to do tomorrow. Daily discipline is **the** key to reaching your goals.
3. Build your life on a solid foundation of honesty, character, faith, integrity, love and loyalty. This foundation will give you an honest shot at reaching any goal you have properly set.
4. Break your Intermediate and Long-Range goals into increments. Examples: I lost 37 pounds by losing 3.7 pounds each month for 10 months, or just 1.9 ounces per day. I wrote *See You at the Top* (348 pages) by writing 1.26 pages per day, every day, for 10 months. (By the mile it's a trial, by the inch it's a cinch!)
5. Shape up mentally, physically and spiritually. It takes energy, mental toughness and spiritual reinforcement to successfully deal with life's opportunities, and to reach your objectives.
   (a) Motivation is the key and a positive attitude is a must, so on a daily basis you should feed your mind with good, clean, pure, powerful and positive material by reading good books and listening to motivational, educational and inspirational recordings. Regularly attend personal growth seminars or industry-related training lectures and training programs. Remember, what you do off the job is going to be a deter-mining factor in how far you go on the job.

(b) Take care of your physical health – proper diet, reasonable sleep, exercise, and eliminate the poisons (alcohol, drugs and tobacco).

(c) Don't let others rain on your parade – or don't be a SNIOP (**S**usceptible to the **N**egative **I**nfluence of **O**ther **P**eople).

6. Be prepared to change. You can't control the weather, inflation, interest rates, Wall Street, etc. Just remember that, at this point, your goals have been **carefully** (and, I hope, prayerfully) set, so change your decision to go, carefully, but be willing to change your direction to get there as conditions and circumstances demand.
7. Share your "give-up" goals (give up smoking, being rude, procrastination, being late, eating too much, etc.) with many people. Chances are excellent they are going to encourage you. Share your "go up" goals (be #1 producer, write a book, graduate with honors and be the class valedictorian, etc.) only with those rare people you strongly feel will give you support and encouragement.
8. Become a team player. Learn to work with a team, such as your family, corporate associates, etc. Remember, "You can have everything in life you want if you will just help enough other people get what they want."
9. See the reaching. In your imagination, see yourself receiving that diploma, getting that job or promotion, making that speech, moving into the home of your dreams, achieving that weight loss goal, building that financial nest egg, etc.
10. Each time you reach a goal, your confidence will grow that you can do bigger and better things. After accomplishing the goal, record the event and cross it off your Things I Really Want to Be, Do or Have sheet.

CRITICAL: *Immediately set a new goal and work that new goal through the General Goals Procedure Chart.*

11. Remember that what you **get** by reaching your destination is not nearly so important as what you will **become** by reaching your goals, because what you will become is the **winner** you were born to be.

NOTE: *Since motivation is critical in the goal-setting and goal-achieving process, it would be helpful if you had our series on goals or our complete "How To Stay Motivated" series.*

IF YOU WANT TO REACH YOUR GOAL, YOU MUST FIRST SEE THE REACHING IN YOUR OWN MIND BEFORE YOU ACTUALLY ARRIVE AT YOUR GOAL.